PRODIGAL OF DEATH

A WESTERN QUINTET

Other Five Star Titles
by T. T. Flynn:

Night of the Comanche Moon
Rawhide
Long Journey to Deep Cañon
Death Marks Time in Trampas
The Devil's Lode
Ride to Glory

PRODIGAL OF DEATH

A WESTERN QUINTET

T. T. FLYNN

Five Star • Waterville, Maine

Five Star First Edition Western Series.

Published in 2001 in conjunction with Golden West Literary
Agency.

Set in 11 pt. Plantin.

Printed in the United States on permanent paper.

Library of Congress Cataloging-in-Publication Data

Flynn, T. T.
    Prodigal of death : a western quintet / by T.T. Flynn.
—1st ed.
      p. cm.
    "Five Star western."
    Contents: Bushwhackers die hard—Killer's guest—
Smart guy—The Pie River—Prodigal of death.
    ISBN 0-7862-2763-X (hc : alk. paper)
    1. Western stories. I. Title.
PS3556.L93 P7 2001
813'.54—dc21   2001023674

TABLE OF CONTENTS

BUSHWHACKERS DIE HARD

T.T. Flynn's agent sold this story to Rogers Terrill, editor of *Dime Western*, on September 25, 1932. The author was paid $240.00 for it, or 1¢ a word. Flynn originally titled the story "The Range Looters," but later changed his mind about that title and came to prefer "Murder Range." The magazine apparently liked neither of these titles and so changed it to "Bushwhackers Die Hard" when the story appeared in the January, 1933 issue of *Dime Western*. The magazine title has been retained for the story's first book edition.

I

"SUDDEN DEATH"

Lonesome Lang straightened abruptly on his big black and burst out: "Look at that fool running them horses! He must be full of liquor or crazy as an addled coyote!"

Forward and up, half a mile away, the narrow, tortuous road the two men were ascending rounded a spur of rock, disappeared in a hairpin curve, and came into sight again at the edge of a dizzy drop. Around that high, distant rock spur a small dust cloud had swirled, racing down toward the next turn. It was a team of horses and a light open buggy. Even as Lonesome pointed, the team dashed into the hairpin curve and vanished from sight.

Tarnation Tucker's mouth gaped beneath his grizzled mustache. He snorted indignantly. "What'n tarnation blazes does thet all-fired idjit think he's doin'? He ain't got no sense a-tall, comin' down such a grade thataway."

Unconsciously the two men had reined up, staring fixedly at the point where the trail came in sight again. Short, tense seconds passed. Abruptly the team of blacks shot into view once more. They were moving fast—too fast, for that steep grade, those abrupt turns. In snapping seconds, every move was etched vividly against the high rocky background. Spurts of dust flew from the hoofs of the off horse as it tried to make the sharp turn and slipped. The two plunging horses collided. The reeling buggy crowded on their flanks. The hoofs of the off horse pounded on the edge, flew out into space, kicking.

"God Almighty, look at that!" Tarnation Tucker gasped.

Both horses were in the air—the light buggy was following them—was turning over. A human figure flew from the seat. Horses, buggy, driver struck the rocky cliff, bounded off, fell, struck again, again—down, down, down. The faint sounds of that ghastly drop ended in one final crash on the rocky floor of the ravine.

Lonesome Lang exhaled through set teeth and sagged back in his saddle. "Wiped out, Tarnation," he breathed. "Deader than a doornail."

Tarnation swiped at his grizzled mustache with the back of his hand, and spat. "Yeah," he muttered, squinting down into the ravine. "Not much chance of comin' through thet. It shore was a crazy stunt."

Lonesome reined his black around. "We better sashay down an' have a look," he suggested.

He was a young man, this Lonesome Lang, tall and spare,

8

with a wide mouth set in a long, homely face, a mouth that had little humorous quirks at the corners and a face whose eyes were sun-wrinkled at the corners, so that Lonesome appeared to be gravely laughing most of the time. A dusty black Stetson was canted at a slight angle over one eye, and a worn calfskin vest hung open over his blue shirt with a frayed Bull Durham tag fluttering from its pocket. An ancient and well-seasoned cartridge belt hung slackly about his middle, holstering a bone-handled Colt .45. Badly scuffed leather chaps, doffed during the day's ride, were tied behind the saddle. A Winchester was thrust into a saddle boot, and the saddle in which he rested easily had the sheen of hard usage and great care. Lonesome Lang was a bit like that saddle himself—worn, scuffed, tanned, hardened, six feet of leathery sinew.

Tarnation Tucker was cast in the same comfortable mold. An old-timer, in his late fifties, with shrewd, squinting eyes set in a wrinkled leathery face that had a trap-like mouth beneath a grizzled mustache. A pearl-handled Colt swung at Tarnation's hip, and worn woolly chaps cased a pair of permanently bowed legs.

Both men were silent as they rode back and sent their horses slipping and sliding down the steep slope of the trail bank.

A few moments later in the boulder-strewn ravine they looked upon the result of that mad ride. It was not a pretty sight. The light buggy had been smashed to matchwood. The smell of blood was in the air. Lonesome's black shied nervously from a crumpled form lying at least a hundred feet from the wrecked buggy. Lonesome dismounted, dropped the reins, and walked over to it.

"Hmm . . . you look old enough to have better sense," he said under his breath as he stared at the crumpled body.

It was a man somewhere near Tarnation's age, white-haired, spare with proud, sharp features. He was clad in a neat black suit, cowman's half-boots inside the trousers. His black hat lay a few feet away.

Lonesome picked up the hat, started to toss it beside the body, and suddenly stared at it fixedly. His lips puckered in a soundless whistle.

Tarnation Tucker, taking in everything with shrewdly narrowed eyes, asked mildly: "See something?"

Lonesome extended the hat, pointed silently to a small round hole in the left side of the crown. He turned it, indicated a duplicate hole on the opposite side.

Tarnation said nothing as he bent over the body and looked closely at the scalp. A grunt of satisfaction came from him as he straightened up. "Huh, might have knowed it. He's creased purty as a wild stallion ever was. Lemme see what his hosses show."

The team was badly scraped and mangled. After a few moments' examination Tarnation grunted again, pointed a gnarled finger at a narrow reddish welt across one flank.

"Rocks never did that. It's plain as the ears on a Sonora burro. He was creased, an' then his team was stung enough to make 'em bust ahead in a crazy run. The trail took care of the rest."

Lonesome tossed the hat beside the owner and nodded. "I didn't hear any shots," he observed thoughtfully. "It must've happened near the top of the rimrock."

"Neither did I. But they was a couple fired sure enough." Tarnation squinted upward. "Rimrock's purty far off. Sound has a way of actin' funny sometimes."

"People, too," Lonesome said dryly. "Now, who'd ever expect a nice-looking old boy like this to be bushwhacked? It just ain't reasonable."

Tarnation spat. "Shore it is. Money, fer one. Bet he's been robbed."

Lonesome felt about the body, brought forth a leather wallet. It had thirty odd dollars in it, and a slip of white paper.

"You're wrong," Lonesome corrected, reading the paper. "He wasn't robbed. An' this paper says he made a deposit this morning at the Vallecito Bank. Whoever bushwhacked him never came near him."

"You're right," Tarnation acknowledged. "Wonder what's behind it?"

Lonesome put the wallet in his pocket. "Hard to tell," he said thoughtfully. "Looks like he's well fixed. He deposited sixty-eight hundred and fifty dollars, accordin' to the slip. Guess we might as well slope along to Vallecito and report it, Tarnation. I'll take his money, just in case some light-fingered gent wanders by and feels obliged to lighten the body. Let's go."

They swung on their saddles again, regained the road, and rode toward the rimrock high above.

The afternoon sun was a fiery ball in the cloudless sky. Lonesome and Tarnation had been riding since dawn. The short hairs of the black and Tarnation's buckskin were frosted with alkali dust. The same dust powdered them both. They rode easily, as men used to grueling distances. The soft click of hoofs on the rocky road, the creak of saddle leather died away on the upper trail. Silence fell over the spot.

The brooding stillness of the rocky cañon bottom was not long undisturbed. Lonesome and Tarnation had hardly passed the rimrock and jogged on their way toward Vallecito when the click of hoofs echoed softly. A lone horseman came riding slowly and cautiously down the cañon. The roan stallion under him was a magnificent animal, rangy and powerful, with a white blaze above his eyes.

The rider's black hat was pulled low over a lean, hatchet face. A close-cropped black mustache covered tight lips. He rode, searching every foot of the cañon bottom, and such glimpses of the winding trail above as could be seen. The wind drifting up the cañon brought the odor of death. The roan stallion shied nervously and snorted. The touch of a large spur rowel drove him on until he stopped, trembling at the spot Lonesome and Tarnation had quitted only a short time before.

For a moment, the rider sat with his hands on the saddle horn, calmly surveying the gruesome spectacle. He seemed neither astonished nor uneasy. Giving a last look down the cañon and up toward the trail above, he dismounted, wrapping the reins about a sinewy hand, in case the roan's nervousness proved too much.

Squatting beside the body, he searched the pockets. A scowl darkened the hatchet face as they proved to be empty. With a muttered oath he straightened up and scanned the ground about with darting glances. He saw the traces of the horses that had so recently been there.

He stepped swiftly to the saddle and jerked a carbine from the leather boot. Alert, wary, he peered down the cañon. The fact that he saw nothing or heard nothing did not reassure him. Leading the roan, he walked slowly forward, studying the faint signs. He came to the spot where Lonesome and Tarnation had descended and ascended again. He replaced the carbine, swung into the saddle, and sent the big roan scrambling up the bank.

On the road it was plain which way Lonesome and Tarnation had gone. The lone rider studied the trail above. Apparently convinced that no one was lurking up there, he rode toward the rimrock. His narrow eyes were blazing, and the carbine was crooked ready in the hollow of his arm.

12

II
"THE RED DOG BAR"

Mountains were lying, hazy and jagged, to the east as Lonesome and Tarnation topped a sandy rise and rode down into Vallecito. The place was a typical southern New Mexico cow town, sprawled on the sandy banks of a small river. The adobe houses seemed to grow out of the dun-colored soil, and giant cottonwoods spread lazy branches among them.

They cantered past the outlying houses, where scantily clad Mexican children played in the dust and sunlight, and came to the heart of town, a small, sleepy plaza. The principal building was a two-story red-brick edifice, with a gold-lettered sign on the front window, marking it as the **Vallecito State Bank.** Lonesome's questing eyes noted a blacksmith's shop in one corner of the plaza, a general store, two saloons.

"Nice little town," he drawled.

"Ain't it?" Tarnation agreed, drowning a black beetle in the dust below and shifting his tobacco to the other side of his mouth. He looked wistfully at the Red Dog Bar to their right. "She's been a dry ride today," he suggested.

Lonesome chuckled. "Every ride is a dry ride to you when we hit town. Won't hurt us to dry out a little more. We got business at the bank first, before she closes."

"Goin' to report what we found? There's the sheriff's office acrost the plaza there."

"Want to see the bank first."

They dismounted at the hitch rack in front of the bank and wrapped their reins around the iron pipe.

"She's a likely lookin' bank," Tarnation commented admiringly as he surveyed the front of the building.

"Ain't she," Lonesome agreed.

The bank building was not new, but about it there was an air of smart success surprising in a town of this kind. The front window was washed and polished until the sun rays struck back in glittering lancets of light. The gold lettering on the windowpane was fresh and new, and the screen door they opened to enter had been freshly painted.

Inside everything was clean, shining, business-like. A banking counter with an iron grill above it divided the room in half. Two windows were set in the grill, and behind one of them stood a thin, withered-looking little man who was peering carefully through steel-rimmed spectacles as he made entries in a ledger. At his right another man sat at a desk, his back to the window.

Lonesome walked to the window.

"I've got a couple of twenty dollar gold pieces I'd like busted smaller," he said, fishing in a pocket. "Some paper and some silver dollars, I reckon."

The little man put the pen down carefully and peered through the wicket at him. "Yes, sir," he said. "Glad to." He pulled out a drawer under the counter, lifted a sheaf of small bills, and began to count them off.

Lonesome asked casually: "Anybody around here named Henry Williams?"

The little man's hand halted in mid-air for the barest instant, as if something had startled him, and then he counted on. His glance slid over the top of the spectacles briefly.

"Henry Williams owns the Lazy H outfit, about ten miles north of town," he stated.

The man at the desk laid down the pen he had been

writing with and swung around. He was short and pudgy with a round, pinkish face and a bald spot on top of his head over which a scattering of black hairs were combed precisely. Glittering rimless eyeglasses perched on his nose, and, despite the slight bulge of his middle and the more mature air of prosperity as he got up and came to the counter, Lonesome judged he was not more than thirty-five. He smiled at Lonesome with lips that were too thin for his well-fed, pinkish face.

"Did I hear you ask for Henry Williams?" he questioned.

"You did," Lonesome admitted.

"Stranger around here?"

"Kind of."

"Always glad to see new faces," said the other genially. "I am Lemuel Stoddard, president of the bank here. Anything I can do for you will be a pleasure, Mister . . . ?"

"Lang," Lonesome told him. "This is my pard, Mister Tucker."

"It's a pleasure, gentlemen," Lemuel Stoddard assured them. "Is there anything I can help you with concerning Henry Williams? He is one of our most valued citizens and customers."

"We have a little business with him," High Lonesome drawled, starting to roll a cigarette.

"Williams has left town for a day or so," Stoddard said. "He stopped in this morning and said he was driving over to Agua Fría."

Lonesome moistened the edge of the cigarette paper, and, as he shaped it and put the end between his lips, the front door of the bank opened, and a young woman hurried to the grilling. Lonesome stepped aside politely and gave her his place. She murmured a word of thanks without actually looking at him.

15

Lonesome lighted his smoke and studied her with appreciation. She was small, slim, straight, with a tumbled mass of wind-blown hair. She wore a short woolen riding skirt and boots, and one hand held a pair of soft leather riding gloves.

"I'd like to get this check cashed, Mister Stoddard," she said briskly, pushing a slip of paper through the window.

Stoddard picked it up, and then put it down again, smiling regretfully. "I'm sorry, Miss Williams. There isn't enough balance in the account to take care of this."

"Not enough? Are you sure?"

The wizened teller smiled thinly and shook his head.

"There must be a mistake," Miss Williams protested. "Dad told me he was going to make a large deposit before he left town. It was understood that I was to check against it."

Stoddard frowned regretfully. "Bowers, did Mister Williams make a deposit while I was out?"

"No," Bowers denied firmly. "He was in here for a few minutes, but he made no deposit. In fact, he said he might want to borrow some before he left town. Business over at Agua Fría, I think. But he didn't come back."

"I must have this check cashed today," the girl insisted. "I don't understand Dad doing a thing like that."

"We have to follow the law in such matters," Stoddard told her regretfully. "The bank examiner is very strict about overdrafts. However, I'll lend you the money for thirty days on your personal note. In fact," said Stoddard gallantly, "any amount you need, Miss Williams. Your father probably forgot it."

"I suppose that will be all right," she agreed doubtfully. "I want a hundred dollars."

Stoddard fished a blank note from under the counter, rapidly filled it in, and slid it and a pen under the wicket. "Just sign on that bottom line."

She signed.

Stoddard counted out a stack of bills himself and pushed them through to her.

"Thank you," she said, taking the money and starting to turn away.

Stoddard glanced at Lonesome, and then said abruptly: "I see you don't know these gentlemen, Miss Williams. This is Mister Lang and Mister Tucker. They were just asking about your father before you came in."

Lonesome swept off his dusty hat and acknowledged her inquiring nod with a duck of his head and a grin. "We drifted down this way for a change," he said. "An' a fellow back on the road said Henry Williams might need a couple of top hands. We figgered to check up on it."

Level, gray eyes surveyed him for a moment, and then the girl shook her head. "I'm sorry. We have all the men we need at present. When Dad comes back in two or three days, you might ride out and see him, if you're in town then."

"Thank you, ma'am. We'll shorely do that," Lonesome assured her. As she turned to the door, he started gathering up his change.

Stoddard pursed his lips. "Looking for work, eh?"

"Sort of."

"Where are you from?"

" 'Most anywheres." Lonesome grinned, pocketing his money. "We sorta drift around. Much obliged for the accommodation, mister." He and Tarnation walked out.

Miss Williams was already riding across the plaza.

Tarnation spat expressively as they mounted and turned away from the bank. "Didja hear thet in there?" he demanded.

"I reckon so. I was there. What was it?"

"Them two sayin' her old man hadn't put no money in the bank today when you had his deposit slip in your pocket all the time. Why didn't you throw down on 'em an' jerk the truth outta their lyin' throats?"

"She got the money, didn't she?"

"What of it? They lied to her. I was figgerin' to do it myself. Le's sashay over to the sheriff an' spill the hull thing to him."

"Let's have a drink," Lonesome suggested. "I want to think. I'm all fogged up."

"Think? You oughta know by now I'm all het up."

Lonesome shook his head dubiously. "I came into town with the idea of turning the money an' deposit slip over to the bank an' telling what we found. But not now, Tarnation. There's something goin' on. Mighty sweet kid, wasn't she?"

"That's just why we oughta do somethin'! Why, her old man's layin' out there in the cañon dead, an' she don't know a thing about it! By Godfrey, I ain't goin' to stand by an'. . . ."

"Hold your horses, Tarnation. We'll do something when we see how the land lays. Here's the Red Dog. Wet your guzzle. It'll help lubricate your brain."

The Red Dog Bar was housed in an old adobe building with a shed roof built out over the dirt walk for shade and the usual hitch rack in front, with five horses lazing before it, champing their bits and stamping flies. Inside, a battered bar was backed by a fly-specked mirror and an assortment of bottles and glasses. Several tables rested about on the sagging floor.

Half a dozen men were lounging at the bar, glasses before them, smoking and talking noisily, when Lonesome and Tarnation entered. The talk stopped abruptly, and the men at the bar turned and eyed the newcomers.

A tall, burly, red-faced man with a gun slung low on his hip and a sagging calfskin vest spoke as they walked to the end of the bar. "Howdy, gents."

"Howdy," said Lonesome amiably. And to the barkeep: "Two slugs of rye."

The man behind the bar, stolid and stocky, with sleeves rolled to his elbows, set out a bottle and glasses.

As Lonesome poured, the red-faced man asked: "Strangers around here?"

"So far," said Lonesome.

"Passin' through?"

"Ef we get in the notion," Tarnation grunted, taking the bottle.

The second man down the bar, a short, compact man with abnormally bowed legs, asked: "You men lookin' for work?"

"Ef we need it," Tarnation replied, slamming the bottle down on the bar. In a voice he did not try to keep low he said to Lonesome: "Funny what a hell of a lot of questions they ask a man in this town."

Lonesome tossed off his drink and, as he set the glass down, answered Tarnation's remark: "Ain't it?"

Then Lonesome leaned an elbow on the bar and surveyed the group calmly as he fished for his tobacco and papers. They were not a likely looking lot. Every man there had the marks of a hard life on his face, and there was no friendliness in their manner. To a man they seemed suspicious, surly.

"Nice-looking range around here," Lonesome drawled. He lighted the cigarette he had rolled and spun the match to the floor. "We might make a visit."

A third man, dour and dark, with black stubble on his cheeks and a battered hat perched far back on his head, said curtly: "There ain't much call for new hands around here. Ef you two want work, you better pull leather to a better place."

19

"Thanks," Lonesome drawled. "You speak like a friend."

"Right. I'm trying to save you time an' trouble."

"Trouble?" Tarnation asked.

"You heard me."

Tarnation snorted and poured himself another drink, muttering between set lips.

Lonesome inhaled and inspected the end of his cigarette. "That sounds like a threat," he said thoughtfully.

"Take it any way you like," said the dour man sullenly.

The swinging doors of the Red Dog Bar had hardly closed behind Lonesome and Tarnation when a sweat-lathered roan stallion with a white blaze above his eyes trotted into the plaza from a different direction than that from which Lonesome and Tarnation had entered town. It made straight for the bank. The rider swung off, dropped the reins, and strode inside.

There were no customers in the bank, no witnesses to what transpired. Only Bowers, the thin, withered cashier, checking his columns of figures behind the iron grillwork glanced silently above his steel-rimmed spectacles as Lemuel Stoddard hurried out from his desk and met the newcomer near the door, and even Bowers was unable to hear what passed between them as they talked in low voices.

Stoddard's plump, pinkish face paled as he listened. He polished his rimless eyeglasses nervously and fitted them back on again with fingers that were not quite steady. He spoke hurriedly, almost breathlessly.

Both men moved to the door and looked out through the glass. Unobserved, Bowers lifted his head and stared at their backs. He saw Stoddard point at something across the plaza, saw the black hat jerk to a curt nod, and then its wearer left the bank as quickly as he had entered. Bowers was writing industriously when Lemuel Stoddard swung around and returned to his desk, biting his underlip until the pale flesh showed the red marks of his teeth.

The atmosphere of the Red Dog was definitely charged with hostility. Lonesome and Tarnation faced five pairs of glowering eyes, and, if they felt any qualms about the trouble that seemed to have flared up over their presence, they did not show it.

Tarnation spat on the floor scornfully.

Lonesome's lips parted in a smile that held little mirth. "I take it you made a threat, mister," he said calmly. "And when a man waves a threat in my teeth, it makes me curious. Who don't want us around here, an' what's going to happen if we stay?"

The burly, red-faced man stepped into the breach with a forced smile. "Shut up, Slicker," he ordered. "Strangers, the boys is a little flighty right now. There's been trouble around here lately. Rustlin', cattle killin', arson and the like, not to speak of bushwhackin'. Folks that don't seem to have no particular business ain't looked on with favor. It's sound advice to move on, no harm meant. Especially when you don't welcome questions. Savvy?"

"I see," Lonesome nodded slowly. His smile grew broader. "That makes it different. But we've covered a heap of ground the last few days, an' Vallecito strikes me just right. There oughta be an opening for two top hands."

"Not with the Railroad brand," said the red-faced man flatly. "These are Railroad hands, and I'm foreman."

"There's others," said Lonesome agreeably.

Before anything more could be said, the swinging doors were shoved in and a rangy, black-mustached man wearing a dusty black Stetson entered and came to the bar. His thin face was expressionless, but his close-lidded eyes studied Lonesome and Tarnation intently.

"Here's the boss now," said the red-faced one calmly. "Mister Crosby, I was just advising these two gents that the Railroad don't need hands, an' they'd better move on."

Crosby stopped and hooked his thumbs in his gun belt. "Strangers around here?" he asked Lonesome.

"We was," Lonesome admitted. "But since we been warned, admonished, an' made unwelcome, not to speak of listenin' to some of the local troubles, we're feelin' at home."

Crosby wore black trousers tucked inside fancy, embroidered half-boots. His shirt was white silk with a flowing, black silk tie, and his dusty black coat was cut cleaner and finer than most coats one found in the cow country. For a cowman he was almost foppish. But there was nothing foppish about the lines of his thin, hatchet face. Lonesome, who had judged men neatly at first sight before, marked imperiousness there, hardness, and for good measure he threw in cruelty.

"Where you been?" Crosby inquired bluntly.

"Vaca Prieta was the last stop, not that it's anybody's business," Lonesome told him shortly.

"Just get in?"

"Yes."

"We can use two men," said Crosby. "Forty a month, and more money if you suit."

"You've hired us," said Lonesome promptly.

"Mebbe we better think it over," Tarnation objected.

"Nope. We need work too bad," Lonesome overruled him. "How do we get to your Railroad bunkhouse?"

"Parr here is your foreman. He'll give you directions as soon as I'm through with him. I want to see you outside a minute, Parr."

The two went out. Lonesome and Tarnation followed a moment later. Crosby and Parr were talking at the hitch rack. The conversation was brief. Crosby jerked his head for Lonesome and Tarnation to join him, and swung on his big roan stallion as they did. From the saddle he said: "If you need anything at the store, Parr will see that you get credit." And with a nod he reined the roan around and rode off.

Less than twenty yards away the daughter of Henry Williams was riding toward them beside a young man. Crosby swept off his Stetson to her. Lonesome saw her chin jerk up haughtily, and she did not acknowledge the greeting. The young man scowled.

Her eyes swept Parr, Tarnation, and himself coldly as she passed. She made no sign that she had ever seen him before.

III
"BUSHWHACKER'S LEAD"

Vallecito lay behind. The sun was a brassy ball in the mid-afternoon sky. To the east the mountains drowsed in a shimmering purple haze. There were low sandy hills covered with greasewood and bunch grass, shimmering white arroyos, parched and dry, and thorny mesquite thickets in which restless whitefaces moved and stared curiously at Lonesome and Tarnation as they walked their horses along the narrow rutted, dusty road.

"It's a danged mess," Tarnation grumbled. "You should've stopped in at the sheriff's an' sent him out to get the body."

"And admit we were there," Lonesome said patiently. "Henry Williams is dead. We can't help him. But maybe we can get to the bottom of things if we keep clear and dumb."

"Whatcha want to hire out to this Railroad outfit for then, an' come clear out here away from town? That bank's the place we want to watch. That slippery Stoddard who lied to the gal."

"Uhn-huh. That's what I thought till Crosby hired us so quick."

"What's he got to do with it?"

"If we knew, we wouldn't have to come all the way out to his ranch to find out. He hired us for a reason. They didn't need hands. His foreman said so. Didn't want strangers. But Crosby took one look at us an' made his play."

"He never seen us before?"

"That's why I'm wondering. He ain't the kind to make a move without a reason. Didja see him get frosted when he met Williams's daughter?"

"She hates his innards. An' she didn't cotton to us when she seen we was with him." Tarnation nodded.

"There you are," Lonesome pointed out. "Henry Williams had enemies. She doesn't have any use for Crosby. If you want to find a snake, where would you look?"

"Damned if I know." Tarnation grunted. "In the first place, I don't want a snake. I had the d.t.s once an' seen too many. All colors. An' ef it's a riddle, I got other things to think about."

"The riddle is who shot Henry Williams, and why? I'm thinkin' the best place to smell him out is through other snakes. We got a den of 'em in the Railroad outfit, or I'm a horny toad."

"Well, you ain't a horny toad," admitted Tarnation reluctantly. "Even if I have called you some lowdown names. So you must be right."

Cr-crack.

There was the thin, sharp spat of a rifle off to their right. Tarnation made a queer sound in his throat and toppled slowly and limply out of his saddle.

The winding road was passing at the moment across the corner of a small alkali flat, with a mesquite thicket some thirty yards to the left and sand hills to the right, sand hills covered with greasewood three feet high, rolling and undulating, cut by narrow, deep arroyos, dry washes, and ledges of rock. It was from the crest of one of these sand hills that the attack had come, marked only by the snap of the shot and Tarnation's reeling fall.

Lonesome threw his right leg over the saddle horn and jerked his rifle from its scabbard as he made a running drop. That action saved his life. For a second shot followed an instant later. He heard the thin, vicious whine of the bullet pass close to his head.

Without stopping to look, Lonesome dove for the nearest mesquite brush in a crouching, zigzag run, a run for his life, for the rifle barked again and again. Lead screamed by him, some of it kicking up angry little fountains of dust just ahead. Before he reached the mesquite, a hammer blow against his side drove him reeling, numbed that side, and seemed to stop heart and breathing for an instant. Stumbling, staggering, carried by the very momentum of his rush, Lonesome plunged into the thorny thickets.

Needle-like mesquite thorns clawed at his body, scratched his face, tore his clothes. Ignoring the damage, he crashed forward, dodged to one side, and threw himself on the ground where dry grass tops and brush made a screen. Her rolled over half a dozen feet, swearing as sharp thorns on the ground thrust into his flesh, and then came to a stop on his stomach, scanning his cover alertly.

It was enough to hide him, Lonesome decided, and a moment later, when the hidden rifle barked again, a bullet whined and flicked through the branches at the spot where he had hunted ground, and he felt that the spot was good enough. Other bullets followed, riddling the brush where he had last been seen, all missing as Lonesome hugged the ground and tried to locate the place where the killer was lurking.

Ordinarily the calmest of men, except when action called, and calm then for the most part, Lonesome was in the grip now of a murderous rage. The first numbing shock in his side had passed, and sharp shooting pains were running up to his shoulder. He could feel the wet seep of blood on his skin. How badly he been hit he did not know, or care at the moment. Tarnation, lying still and crumpled there in the dust of the road, wiped everything else from his mind. Tarnation who always gave the other fellow a break—had been cut down now without a chance by a hidden killer.

The dirty, scabby, cold-blooded snake. Lonesome gulped thickly. *I'll get his guts if I have to walk up an' tear 'em out with my bare hands. Show yourself, you snake!*

But the shots had ceased. Quiet fell over the spot. Ominous quiet. The sun blazed overhead. The mesquite thicket was hot, and little shimmering heat waves danced in the air. Lonesome could see Tarnation's legs in the road, one knee drawn slightly up, motionless, dreadfully motionless.

A horse stamped down the road, and bit chains jangled softly. That would be Spade, Tarnation's horse. Frosty, his own black, would be around somewhere, too. Both horses were used to gunfire and gentled to stay close when their reins were dropped.

Lonesome had lost his hat. He raised his bare head an inch at a time until he could look through the thin top of his screen, through the intervening mesquite branches and see the sandy rise beyond the road.

He waited, watching. A breeze above the ground ruffled the slender branches of the greasewood on the hill's crest. Lonesome's eyes searched without luck for the glint of sun on a rifle barrel, for a sudden movement that would betray the gunman.

Three small birds flew swiftly over the hilltop, and veered suddenly off to the side and vanished. It would have been insignificant to almost anyone else, but to Lonesome it meant much. Something had alarmed those birds. Something just over the crest of the hill where he could not see. He watched the spot.

A few moments later he saw a slight movement there, then the slow, snake-like thrusting motion of a rifle barrel around the edge of a boulder. A head and shoulders followed, and the man fell still, intently scanning the road and the mesquite beyond.

Stealthily Lonesome drew up a knee, braced himself, and raised his rifle. A long moment he cuddled it to his shoulder, drawing the sights full on the spot, then gently squeezed the trigger. The instant the shell exploded, he pumped another in and jerked the rifle to firing position again. There was a sudden flurry in the greasewood. A half revealed torso lurched up. Lonesome fired again.

The figure tumbled back out of sight, dragging the rifle barrel above the greasewood as it went. Lonesome threw himself over to one side, but no shot came. When he looked again, the trembling branches at the spot were quieting, and stillness hung over the alkali flat, the electric stillness of destruction—and death.

Lonesome waited. It was all he could do. He did not know how badly he had hit the fellow, or if he had hit him at all. The distance was a full hundred and twenty-five yards, too great even to see clearly the features that had peered in his direction. There might be another ambush, the man more patient this time.

Five minutes passed. Slow, dragging, tense minutes. . . .

Suddenly Lonesome swayed his head and stared unbelievingly, stared with pounding heart and a growing lump of hope in his throat. Tarnation's foot had moved. Then the other leg. He saw Tarnation sit up with an effort. A reckless shout burst from him. "Tarnation! You all right?"

"Hell, no, I ain't all right!" Tarnation's shaky voice replied testily. "I got a face full of blood an' a hell of a headache. Where in tarnation are you? What happened?"

"I'm over here in the mesquite."

Tarnation staggered upright and weaved there a moment until he got his balance. "What in Hades are you doin' over there in the mesquite?" he called. "Have you turned cow critter an' run in the brush to get shet of the flies? Come out an' tell me who throwed me down in the road an' kicked my face."

No shot had been fired at Tarnation since he had moved, which would have happened if a rifle had been covering him. Lonesome got to his feet and walked warily out, picking up his hat as he went.

Tarnation said: "Well, for the love of polecats an' piñons . . . you look like forty wildcats got you down and started scratchin'. You're a terrible sight."

"You ain't such a beauty yourself." Lonesome grinned. "Your face would look at home in the slaughter line at a packing house."

Tarnation's countenance was liberally smeared with

drying blood, and there was an angry red scar across the front of his forehead. He limped, as he moved, and rubbed his shoulders ruefully. "I been tromped on," he said with conviction. "Assaulted an' tromped on, by Godfrey. An' I can't even remember it. What busted up our peaceful *pasear?*"

"Bushwhacked," said Lonesome briefly, and, watching the top of the sand hills warily, he told Tarnation what had happened. "Must have just pinked you in the head, instead of ventilating your brains," he finished. "And me. I drew one in the side as I hightailed for cover."

Lonesome jerked out his shirt and bared his side as he spoke. There was plenty of blood in evidence, and a raw scar across one rib. The spot was sore and painful, but after a quick examination he nodded with relief. "Bounced off a rib," he said. "Poured a little blood, but I'm all right."

"Too ornery to kill," Tarnation grumbled. "An' you say you got the snake what done it?"

"I think so. He flopped back pretty wild."

"Lemme get my rifle an' we'll go see. Guess you did ef he hasn't cut loose on us by now."

Their horses were a hundred yards or so down the road, nipping at the scanty grass off side. Tarnation got his rifle and came back, his wrinkled, leathern face grim and his shrewd eyes narrowed and cold.

Spreading out a few paces, guns ready in their hands, they walked across the flat ground to the base of the hill and climbed it. Their advance was not disputed. A few moments later they were standing at the spot where Lonesome had spotted the ambusher.

They could see the marks on the ground behind the boulder where he had lain. Empty shells were scattered to one side. There were deep boot marks in the soft gravel soil. But of the man himself there was no sign.

"Look," said Lonesome, pointing to the ground.

Large drops of blood were spaced along the footprints.

"You sure got him good," said Tarnation with satisfaction. "He's spoutin' gore like a stuck pig."

The footprints led down into the narrow arroyo at the base of the hill, and there they found where a horse had been standing. More blood stained the ground there, and the hoof marks led back up the arroyo, growing farther apart and deeper as the animal increased his pace.

"Let's foller the pup," Tarnation urged angrily. "I aim to get one shot at him. Jest one is all I ask."

"And maybe get ambushed again for our trouble," Lonesome pointed out. "He's heading back in the sand hills there. No telling how far away he is now. We can't see fifty yards ahead anywhere. He may be laying for us. And next time he'll shoot closer. Let him go."

"I reckon you're right," Tarnation agreed after a moment's thought. "But I shore hate to do it. Every time my head hurts, my trigger finger itches."

They discussed the matter as they walked back to the road. "It was a low-down dirty trick," said Tarnation angrily. "I don't get the idea. Ef that's the kind of country this is, no wonder folks is told to move on."

"Somebody was laying for us," Lonesome said thoughtfully. "And laying to kill. That wasn't a hold-up, or a warning. The first shot would have stopped you for good if it had been an inch back. And he sure wasted lead trying to get me."

"Why go after our scalps? We don't know anyone."

"We've met a few."

"Who knowed we was coming out this way?" Tarnation demanded.

"Parr . . . Crosby . . . the Railroad boys."

"Huh . . . couldn't 'a' been them. We been hired to work with 'em."

"We've been hired," Lonesome corrected. "Crosby didn't say what for. An' I'm betting it wasn't to ride cows. Didn't Parr tell us they didn't need riders?"

"He ain't the boss."

"He's foreman, evidently."

"We left town ahead of 'em. Idea . . . as I got it . . . they were stayin' in until evening."

"We rode slow and weren't there to see who stayed and who didn't."

They reached their horses and mounted. Tarnation gnawed off a generous hunk of chewing tobacco and stowed it in his cheek. "Ef you think the Railroad outfit knowed about this," he said bluntly, "ain't we two fools to go sashayin' in tuh them? Like a couple pore bugs walkin' smack into a tarantula's burrow."

"I reckon we're fools to stop off in Vallecito at all," Lonesome admitted. "But as long as we're fools, we might as well go whole hog. An' don't forget Henry Williams, and that girl of his."

IV

"BRAND BLOTTERS"

The Railroad range lay toward the base of the mountains that sprawled to the east of Vallecito. Headquarters, at the end of the narrow-rutted road, was along the banks of a small stream that came rushing down out of a large mountain cañon to meander aimlessly in a sandy channel when it reached the valley. Towering cottonwoods ringed the bank where the ranch buildings lay. The big house was a low adobe, sand-plastered, with a long *portal* whitewashed inside, and thick fortress-like walls and small windows. Down the creekbank from it was the bunkhouse, corrals, and a windmill. The whole place was in good repair, successful and prosperous.

Lonesome looked around with approval as they rode up. "Crosby's a good cowman," was his verdict.

"Which don't fasten any angel's wings on his shoulders," said Tarnation dryly. "Let's git settled an' wait for the lightnin' to strike."

It was after dark when the men came from town, riding hard, laughing, singing, whooping. Crosby wasn't with them, and the welcome Lonesome and Tarnation got was not cordial. In the bunkhouse, after the horses had been put up, the dour, dark Slicker said to Lonesome: "Where'd you say you come from today?"

"Vaca Prieta."

"You hit the rimrock west of town 'bout noon, I reckon?"

"I reckon," Lonesome agreed.

"Pass a buggy on the road?"

"No," said Lonesome truthfully. "Why?"

"They found a buggy down in the cañon below the rimrock. Went over one of the turns. Kilt the fellow who was driving it. Henry Williams of the Lazy H."

Lonesome was splicing in the hondo of his lariat. He rested it on a knee and raised one eyebrow at Slicker. "That so? We saw his daughter in the bank. Was wondering if they needed a couple of hands on the Lazy H. She said to see her old man when he came back. This'll be tough on her. How'd he come to drive over? Drunk?"

Lonesome was conscious of every eye in the room on him

and Tarnation, watching their faces.

"That's what they're wonderin'," Slicker said significantly. "He was robbed of a heap of money he was carrying, an' there's the marks of three hosses that had been down to the body."

Lonesome looked at Tarnation inquiringly. "See anything of three riders after we left Vaca Prieta?" he asked.

"Nary a sign," denied Tarnation. He heaved a gusty sigh through his gnarled mustache. "An' to think that pore devil was lyin' down there below the road when we rode up it. Must have, or we'd've met his buggy. I shore hope they get the snakes who done it."

"You two looked pretty well clawed up," commented another one of the men. "You wasn't that way when you left Vallecito."

"Someone must've declared open season on travelers today," Lonesome remarked dryly. "We was bushwhacked. Shot Tarnation out of his saddle and run me into the mesquite brush. But there was only one. I shot him up considerable, an' he hightailed. You men didn't happen to see a wounded man, did you?"

Thick silence fell for a moment. Slicker said slowly: "Nope. We didn't see no one." But Lonesome got the feeling that they were holding something back behind that silence.

Tarnation asked casually: "Where's Parr? He didn't come back with you, did he?"

"He stayed in town, I reckon," Slicker said sullenly. "Boys, I'm tired. Reckon I'll hit the soogans."

Nothing more was said about the death of Henry Williams during the next few days, but Lonesome and Tarnation got the impression that they were being constantly watched. Few words were spoken to them, and then only in the order of work. They were two men apart from the rest.

Parr, the foreman, did not return. No explanation was made of his absence. Crosby gave what orders there were to give in the times he was at the ranch. He was away almost as much as he was at home.

In all there were twelve or thirteen men riding out of the Railroad headquarters. More than the place needed, Lonesome decided, and they were handled queerly. The spring roundup was long over, the fall roundup months away, and yet most of the men were out on mysterious business.

Once in the middle of the night, a group of strange riders appeared at the ranch house, changed horses, and left at once. The horses they left were still weary and drooping the next morning. No one said anything about the mysterious visit, but Lonesome noticed that he and Tarnation were under particular scrutiny that morning.

They got little news from the town and country around. They might have been prisoners and the rest of the Railroad outfit their jailers for all the information they were able to pick up. And the tension grew greater as the Railroad men seemed to grow surlier. Twice while Lonesome and Tarnation were riding out, they saw signs that they were being followed.

Tarnation fretted. "We ain't gettin' nowhere," he complained. "They're watchin' us like a flock of buzzards expectin' a kill. I keep lookin' for a knife in the back, or another bushwhackin' job."

"So do I," Lonesome confessed. "Crosby ain't keeping us out here for his health or ours."

"You still got that deposit slip?"

"Yes. And Williams's pocketbook, too."

"We ought to take them to his daughter an' talk it over with her. Mebbe she can tell us some things we ought to know."

"Wait a day or so," Lonesome conceded.

But the next day saw their vague plans brought suddenly to a head. Crosby ordered them to ride out northeast toward the base of the mountains, and bring in any horses they found.

Mid-morning found them miles from the home corral, riding in the foothills, where piñons and small junipers dotted the roughly rolling ground. Such horses as they found they were hazing down out of the brush and throwing them together. Suddenly Lonesome heard the angry bawling of a cow some distance ahead. It continued for several moments, and then without warning a rifle cracked sharply at the spot.

Lonesome rode swiftly in that direction. Some distance away Tarnation was already doing the same. As Lonesome topped a juniper-covered ridge, he suddenly reined in with an oath on his lips, and then rode swiftly down into the grassy hollow ahead. For a riderless horse was mincing around down there, a lariat stretched tautly from its saddle horn to the hind legs of a cow. The cow was bawling and trying to rise, but the well-trained pony was keeping the rope taut and frustrating her attempts. But that was not what had brought the oath to Lonesome's lips.

Sprawled on the ground near the horse was the limp figure of a man. A young man, Lonesome saw as he rode up and leaped to the ground. The man's face was covered with blood, and his chest was rapidly soaking red. He was pale and unconscious. The blood on his face was coming from a large deep gash over one eye. The chest wound lay beneath a small, round hole through coat and shirt. A bullet hole. Lonesome had seen the young man before, riding the Vallecito plaza beside the daughter of Henry Williams.

Tarnation galloped up and dismounted, whistled softly as he looked down at the victim. "Is he dead?" he demanded.

"Looks like he hit his head on that stone when he keeled out of the saddle and got knocked unconscious. Get your rifle out and scout for the fellow who did this, Tarnation."

Neither of them ever left the ranch house without his rifle, unmindful of how it would look. Tarnation mounted again and rode cautiously to the top of the rise, and began to circle around the spot.

Lonesome ripped the shirt open and hurriedly examined the wound. It was in the shoulder, under the collar bone, and he couldn't tell whether the lung had been punctured or not. The bullet had blasted through, ripping out a larger hole in the back. The openings were bleeding badly. He did the best he could, ripping up his neckerchief and wadding it into the holes to stop the flow of blood.

Tarnation circled the hill crest while he was doing that, and finally shouted: "Here's where he stood." He dismounted, picked something off the ground, swung into the saddle again, scanned the country around, and then galloped back. His face was grim as he jumped off.

"He rode hard from there," said Tarnation. "Reckon there's no use follerin' him unless we want to leave this young feller here to die. I got the empty shell from his rifle. How bad is it?"

"Pretty bad," said Lonesome. "You recognize this fellow?"

"Placed him soon as I rode up," said Tarnation. "He was riding with the girl the other day when Crosby spoke to them. An' he acted like Crosby was dirt. What's he doing here on Railroad range, ropin' Railroad cattle? It looks funny."

Lonesome frowned as he turned his head and stared at the cow, which was still trying to get up. "Maybe it isn't a Railroad cow," he said, and walked over to look.

The Railroad brand was on the flank, but when he saw it

close up, Lonesome called Tarnation over.

"Look," he said. "Part of the brand is fresh."

"An' the old brand makes a Lazy H!" Tarnation exclaimed. "Say, ain't we been fools not to think of that before? Ef anybody had studied out a brand that would take the Lazy H easy, he couldn't have done better'n the Railroad. Both of 'em has got the side rails. Run a top an' bottom cross-tie an' pull out the middle line of the H, an' you've got a perfect Railroad with three cross-ties."

"I guess that explains what a Lazy H rider is doing with a Railroad cow on the ground," Lonesome declared. "He was verifying some suspicions. Somebody was watching him and shot him down."

"We got to get him to some care," Tarnation said as they swung back to the body.

"Not Crosby's house," Lonesome said swiftly. "I'm thinkin' this'll make trouble. The fellow who shot him probably figgers he's dead. I guess he meant to turn the cow loose, but didn't stop for that when he heard us coming. It had to be a Crosby man who did it. If we bring the young fellow in, it mightn't be so healthy for all three of us."

"The nearest place is the Lazy H, then," Tarnation judged. "It's about straight west of here. A lot nearer than tryin' to get him into town."

"It'll be a hard ride."

"No worse'n keeping him here on the ground till he bleeds to death. Tell you what, ef you can handle him, I'll ride on ahead an' try to get things ready."

"That's best, I guess," Lonesome agreed. "Help me tie him on his horse and turn that cow loose. Can't haze her along for evidence now."

"She'll be around in the brush," Tarnation said, "and likely others, too."

They bandaged up the wounded shoulder as well as they could. Just as they finished, the victim mumbled something and opened his eyes.

He was a young man in his early twenties. His face had the pallor of the cities, and his boots, Stetson, and Levi's were new, but he had roped the cow neatly. His features were thin, with high cheek bones and a squarish, stubborn chin. When he saw them bending over him, he swore with an Eastern accent.

"You dirty gunmen . . . ," he gasped weakly. "Shooting at me from cover like that."

"Hey-ah . . . hold your hosses, son! We didn't shoot you," Tarnation denied hastily.

"No? You damn' cow thieves would lie about that, too, I guess." The young man launched into a business-like cursing, effective despite his weakness.

"Ain't he the word-slinger, though?" Tarnation grinned admiringly. "All right, son, have your say. We ain't got time to argue. Got to get you to a doctor. Feel able to ride a little?"

The victim was stronger now and, with Lonesome's assistance, was sitting up, wincing at the pain in his shoulder. "Ride where?" He glared suspiciously.

"To the Lazy H. An', by the way, what's your name?"

"You know damned well what my name is! And if you think you can fool me by pretending to take me to the Lazy H, you have another think coming!" The young man's hand abruptly hauled the revolver from the holster at his side.

Lonesome knocked it aside, and it exploded harmlessly in space. Lonesome twisted the gun away.

"You young fool," he said grimly. "We're trying to help you. Trying to get you back to a doctor. Now stop this foolishness. You can cuss it out of your system after you get fixed up."

There was no more resistance. They lifted him into his saddle. Lonesome mounted, and Tarnation led his horse over and slipped the lass rope off the cow. As she scrambled to her feet and charged Tarnation, he rode nimbly out of the way, leading her off.

Lonesome and his charge began to ride into the west. A few minutes later Tarnation passed them at a gallop, shouting: "Good luck! See you both later!"

That was a ride Lonesome never forgot—two steadily pacing horses, up hill and down, through steep-banked arroyos and across sandy washes, the sun blistering and parching, and the sullen, pain-racked young man refusing to talk. His wound bled from the incessant jolting. There was nothing Lonesome could do to stop it, save to stop now and then and adjust the bandage.

The young man grew steadily weaker. Finally he grew delirious and began to talk to himself, and laugh, and now and then to jeer at Lonesome. Lonesome rode close, watching his charge every instant, so as to be ready to catch him if he started to tumble from the saddle. Half a dozen times, in fact, he did just that, having to brace the rapidly weakening victim, and they plodded on.

When they were a mile from the state road, a buckboard, madly driven, approached them. A hard-bitten man in Levi's and blue shirt was driving. Henry Williams's daughter sat on the seat beside him. Three other riders and Tarnation, on a fresh horse, accompanied them.

Little was said as the delirious victim was taken down and laid on a pile of quilts in the buckboard. They started on, one of the men leading the riderless horse.

"We might as well go with 'em," Tarnation said to Lonesome. "I told how we found him, but they didn't take it so favorable. The boy's her cousin. Out here for the summer. Guess he comes every summer."

A doctor from Vallecito, sent for as soon as Tarnation first reached the ranch, arrived in an automobile a few minutes after they got in. Lonesome and Tarnation sat out on the *portal* of the long, low adobe ranch house and smoked and waited. The three riders were all that were in evidence around the place. They drew off to themselves and asked no questions. After a long period the doctor came out, glanced at them curiously, and said cheerfully to Miss Williams who followed him: "I think he'll be all right, Miss Leslyn. Change those bandages like I told you, and I'll be back late tonight or early in the morning."

He went out to his automobile and drove away, and Leslyn Williams faced them there on the *portal*, brushing the hair back from her cheeks as she spoke icily. "I suppose I should thank you for bringing Harry home . . . after you shot him."

"Miss, we didn't shoot him," Lonesome denied. "We found him just after he was shot."

"Harry says you did."

"He never seen who plugged him," Tarantion broke in.

"It was one of Crosby's men," she blazed.

"Reckon that's right." Lonesome nodded.

"And you're Crosby's men. I saw you in town with him that day you tried to get work with us. Spies, I suppose, that Crosby was trying to plant here. And when that wouldn't work, you were brazen enough to go right over to him."

She was scornfully angry, and pretty as a picture, Lonesome thought, with her cheeks blazing and her slender shoulders thrown back.

"You're all upset, miss," Tarnation soothed. "We never seen Crosby before until after Lonesome here talked to you."

"Do you expect me to believe that?"

Lonesome shook his head and fingered the brim of his hat. "I don't reckon I do, with the way things are," he said. "You're having trouble here, ain't you?"

"You should know all about it," she said bitterly.

"But we don't. Except that you been losin' cattle."

"So you do know that?"

"Your cousin had roped a Railroad cow just before he was plugged," Lonesome explained. "Tarnation an' me saw the Railroad brand had been made over from a Lazy H, and not long ago, either. It didn't take much to get at the truth of that. You've been losin' cattle, haven't you?"

For a moment Leslyn Williams faced him with blazing cheeks and defiant air, and then moisture appeared in her eyes and her small chin quivered. "We've been losing cattle all year," she admitted unsteadily, "and having trouble of every kind. Our alfalfa was burned last winter. Our windmills out away from the house have been tampered with until we're never sure of water. Our men seem to get in trouble all the time. It's been terrible. And other ranchers have suffered the same way. Dad finally decided to go to Agua Fría and get gunmen to protect his rights. And . . . and on the way he was killed. It was murder. Cowardly murder. And they couldn't even wait until he was buried before they were at it again. We lost twenty head. Harry rode out to check what Dad had suspected and could never prove, and got shot for his trouble. Crosby's outfit has been stealing our cattle and changing the brands to their Railroad brand all along. We haven't got half as many cattle as we had this time last year. The bank holds a heavy mortgage on the ranch, and I suppose I'll lose it now that the money Dad had is gone. They've already notified me the mortgage is coming due. But I'll fight first!"

Leslyn Williams clenched her small fists and faced Lonesome and Tarnation defiantly. "I'll fight," she repeated. "As

Dad would have! Go back and tell Crosby that. Tell him I'm going into town and swear out a warrant for him as quickly as I can."

Lonesome's gaze held compassion. "We ain't goin' back," he told her. "We've been eating Crosby's grub because we knew there was something sour around here and thought we could find the answer to it over there. But now we're on your side of the fence for Crosby an' everyone to see."

"You . . . you expect me to believe that? What reason have you to do it?"

"None," admitted Lonesome. "Except we figured the other day in Vallecito that you were drawin' a raw deal from someone, an' we thought we might stick around and do something about it. And Crosby seemed the likeliest place to locate for pay dirt."

"I don't understand."

Before Lonesome could say anything more the drumming beat of hard-ridden horses sounded suddenly at the side of the house. Crosby, at the head of seven of his men, burst into view. They swung around before the *portal* in a cloud of dust and reined up sharply. Crosby leaped to the ground and strode to the porch, his men behind him.

Lonesome stared with narrowing eyes, and did not answer Tarnation's hushed: "Now what the hell are they doing here?"

Leslyn Williams met Crosby with lifted chin and blazing eyes. "What do you want here, Mister Crosby?" she demanded coldly.

Crosby was dressed at his foppiest, silk shirt and flowing tie, handmade riding boots polished neatly, pearl-handled revolver in a silver-studded holster at his hip, and his sombrero at a jaunty angle. On his thin hatchet face there was an apologetic smile as he swept off his sombrero. "This is a sad visit, Miss Williams," he said regretfully. "I wish it could have been under other circumstances. I learned a little while ago that your cousin had been shot on my land. And I rode over at once to settle the matter."

"How did you find out?" Lonesome snapped.

"Slicker saw it," Crosby told him coldly, "and rode in to the ranch house at once and told me. And we've come for you two, Lang. *Raise your hands!*"

Crosby's pearl-handled .45 leaped from its holster and covered Lonesome and Tarnation. His men drew their belt guns, also.

V
"COME SHOOTING"

The thing was so unexpected that Lonesome was caught off guard. Tarnation, also. Before he knew what was coming, he was looking into Crosby's muzzle. In Crosby's cold eyes he saw that which made him lift his hands. They were the eyes of a killer. Murder was flaming there.

"I . . . I don't understand," Leslyn Williams stammered.

"You can't be expected to," Crosby told her. "I suppose these men came here with a fancy tale about finding your cousin wounded on the ground and succoring him?"

"Why . . . why, yes. They said someone else had shot him."

"They lied," said Crosby flatly. "My man saw the whole thing. And being one against two he came in for help."

Slicker was standing back with the other men. His dour face twisted in a sardonic sneer as Lonesome looked at him angrily.

Tarnation swelled until it seemed he might burst. "You mean you're layin' that dirty trick on us?" he snapped at Crosby.

"I'm seeing that you two gunmen don't get away with it," Crosby retorted coolly. "Not on my ranch. I've suspected you ever since you asked me for work, and now this confirms it."

"But they brought Harry home," Leslyn said uncertainly. "Why should they do that if they shot him?"

"To curry favor with you," Crosby told her. "They probably lost their nerve at the last moment."

"You're a cold-blooded liar, Crosby," Lonesome rasped. "And if you didn't have a gun on me, I'd smash the words down your dirty throat."

"I've suspected these men ever since I heard your father had been killed out on the Vaca Prieta road," Crosby told Leslyn Williams. "They came past there about the time he was killed. I've been watching them to see if they'd give themselves away. Boys, this is as good a time as any to make sure. Search them and see what you find."

Too late Lonesome realized the trap that had snapped on them. If he had known it was coming, he could have forestalled it. If Crosby had arrived a few minutes later, the burden of evidence could have been with him. But now it was too late.

"Don't none of you men put a hand on me," he warned thickly.

"Search them," Crosby ordered. "Get their guns first. I'll stop them if they start trouble."

Lonesome saw Crosby's finger tense over the trigger of his gun. Crosby was waiting for the merest excuse to plug him. Lonesome didn't give him that excuse. He stood with his hands high and a bitter smile on his mouth while Crosby's men tramped up, took their guns, and two of them hurriedly searched him, and two searched Tarnation. They found Lonesome's money belt under his shirt. One of them unbuckled it and handed it to Crosby, who looked in the pockets quickly. He took out a black wallet and opened it.

At sight of that wallet Leslyn drew in her breath with a little gasp. "That's Dad's!" she cried.

"Yes," Crosby nodded. "It's your father's. Here's his name stamped inside it. And this is probably some of his money, too."

"He should have had a lot of money," she faltered. "He left here with hundreds of dollars. He was going in to the bank at Vallecito to meet the mortgage."

"They've probably hidden the rest," Crosby shrugged. "But these are the men who ambushed your father and brought about his death. The sheriff has been looking for them hard. This evidence is good enough to hang them."

Leslyn Williams shrank away from Lonesome. Loathing was in her gaze, and then blazing fury. "You . . . you thieving murderer," she choked. "You came here saying you were trying to help me. And all the time you were carrying that wallet you took off my father's dead body. Oh . . . I hope they hang you quick."

"Miss," said Lonesome desperately, "it ain't true."

"I can see with my own eyes! You not only killed him, but you got away with most of the money he had scraped together to meet his notes at the bank."

"I know the evidence looks pretty bad," Lonesome argued. "But I was just getting ready to tell you about it when Crosby rode up."

"I wouldn't believe a thing you said if you swore on the Bible!" she cried.

Lonesome did not argue with her further. She was in no state to listen to reason now. He had been watching Crosby out of the corner of his eye. Crosby had looked all through the wallet and the money belt. An irritated little frown was etched between his eyes.

"Search them again," Crosby ordered one of his men. "Let's see everything they've got on them." He moved closer as the man obeyed, gun held ready.

While Tarnation spluttered in helpless rage, Lonesome stood there with his hands up and his face blank and cold. His expression did not change when the search brought to light only a few minor objects, but, as he watched Crosby, in his eyes was a glint of cold humor.

Crosby gnawed his underlip and scowled. "Sure that's all that's on them?" he demanded harshly.

"That's all, boss."

"Expecting something else, Crosby?" Lonesome asked softly.

Crosby gave him a black look as he spoke. "Miss Williams, we're going to take them to town and charge them with the murder of your father. You'll back that up, of course?"

"I will!" Her face was white and set as she met Lonesome's steady gaze.

"I suppose you know, miss," said Lonesome slowly, "that Crosby doesn't intend to reach town? He'll cook up some shenanigan about our trying to escape, and that'll be the end of it."

Her dislike of Crosby sobered her for a moment. "Why shouldn't he want you to get to town?" she asked swiftly.

"Well, there's the matter of the Lazy H brand bein' blotted. And I expect he can name others."

"If there's been any brand blotting done around here, you two are at the bottom of it!" Crosby charged harshly. "You two have evidently come in here to make trouble. I don't know what's back of it. But you're going to hang for the killing and robbing of her father!"

"If you were to come in with us, miss, Crosby couldn't play his hand," Lonesome suggested.

Her face brightened. "I have to watch the man you shot. I don't know what you're up to, but I won't be a party to it. Crosby can take you in to the sheriff without my help."

"That's right, Miss Williams." Crosby grinned. "Boys, take them out and put them on their horses. And watch them. They're hard customers." Crosby stepped back, holstering his gun with a self-satisfied sneer under his small black mustache.

Lonesome, standing with his hands over his head, felt his spirits drop. Crosby held all the cards. Any defense they offered would be instantly checkmated by Crosby. It did not even look as if they were going to be tied up. Bound men could not be charged with escape so easily.

Tarnation was watching him fixedly. Lonesome moved one eyelid slightly. Tarnation twitched an eyelid back. That was enough. They understood each other.

Lonesome's right hand flashed to the crown of his hat, and the same motion, so quick the eye could hardly follow it, dashed the hat at the eyes of the man who had searched them and now had out his gun. The fellow saw the movement, swung instinctively to meet it. Blinded by the hat across his eyes, he tried to shoot Lonesome down.

Lonesome's big hand knocked the gun aside. The bullet went wild toward Crosby's other men. They instinctively ducked and scattered.

Crosby grabbed for his gun with an oath. But Tarnation had moved with the speed of a grizzled old snake. His hand shot from behind and plucked the gun from Crosby's holster.

With his left hand Lonesome grabbed the gun he had knocked aside and swung his right fist from the hip. It smashed into the man's jaw with a sickening crunch, jarring Lonesome's arm to the shoulder, but it lifted the other off his heels and slammed him back against the house wall. He bounced limply and pitched to the floor of the porch, knocked cold. Lonesome whirled around with the revolver.

Tarnation was jamming Crosby's gun into Crosby's back. Lonesome faced Crosby's men out beyond the porch in a fighting crouch, his thumb holding back the gun hammer.

Leslyn Williams had slipped hurriedly aside with a gasp. Now she whirled in the door to run inside.

"Stay here, miss! Don't go for your men if you don't want 'em hurt!" Lonesome warned sharply without turning his head. He addressed Crosby's men. "You boys wanted trouble, and now you've got it. If you're coming, come shootin'!"

"An' come shootin' fast, you damned thievin' blotters!" Tarnation shouted. " 'Cause I'm itchin' fer an excuse to throw lead in this snake afore I start on the rest of you!"

"Stand still, boys," Crosby begged hoarsely. "They're watching for a chance to kill me. Don't go for your guns."

Crosby's men paid heed.

Leslyn Williams stared at Lonesome scornfully. "And you wanted me to believe you're innocent!" she threw at him. "I suppose you're using me, also, to keep them from shooting?"

"Now that's a thought," Lonesome agreed. "You might come closer and make it safer." He stepped over to her and laid a hand on her shoulder.

She struck it away. "Keep your hands off me, you . . . you cowardly killer."

"Bring him inside," said Lonesome to Tarnation, "and let him have it if his men start anything. Crosby, tell your men to stand out here in front peaceable while we make ourselves comfortable inside."

"You heard him, men," Crosby choked. "There's nothing I can do."

Tarnation hauled Crosby inside. Lonesome followed with Leslyn Williams. He kicked the door shut, ran his hand over Crosby, and retrieved the black wallet.

"That's my father's. I want it."

"Can't have it," Lonesome refused.

"You . . . you thief!"

"Yes, miss. I reckon I seem so."

"What'll I do with this snake? Pistol-whip the truth outta him?" Tarnation growled as he shook Crosby by the collar.

"Nope. Don't hurt him. Bring him to the back of the house. Show us the back door, miss."

Leslyn did that in icy silence. Lonesome looked out. Their horses were back near the corral where they had left them. Another horse was also tied there. "Come along, miss." He led the way swiftly to the corral.

Their rifles were still in the saddle boots. Lonesome unbuckled Crosby's gun belt and hooked it over his saddle horn. "Climb on that horse, Crosby," he ordered curtly.

"What are you going to do?" Crosby demanded, lifting his lower lip nervously.

"Take a little *pasear*. Climb up. Get up and watch him, Tarnation."

As Crosby went in the saddle, Lonesome swung up on his own horse. A flashing smile lit his angular features for a moment as he looked down at the set, scornful face of the girl.

"So long," he said to her. "Don't think too hard of us, miss."

They rode hard from the corral as one of Crosby's men, stepping to the corner of the house, saw them and shouted to the others. Crosby rode between them, his face black and sullen, his eyes going nervously to the guns in the hands of

Lonesome and Tarnation. The man obviously expected violence.

They were followed, of course. But when they were well away from the house, Lonesome drew the rifle from the boot and sent a shot whining back over the pursuers. The men promptly lagged out of sight in that rough, rolling country.

They rode north, away from the Lazy H and Vallecito. Rode hard. When they had put five full miles behind them, Lonesome drew up on top of a rise and scanned the country behind. He saw no sign of the pursuit, but he knew it was there, dogging their tracks.

"Get down, Crosby," he directed.

Crosby's face was white as he did so. He gulped fearfully as he stared up at Lonesome.

"I oughta kill you right here," Lonesome said thoughtfully.

"You . . . you wouldn't do that!" Crosby begged hoarsely. "I haven't got a chance."

"Which is more than you deserve, anyway," Tarnation rasped. "Let's settle up right here, Lonesome."

Lonesome shook his head. "We're leaving you here, Crosby," he said coldly. "We're riding north. You've made it too hot around here for peaceful men. Maybe you'll come after us. But I wouldn't, Crosby. Some of you will get hurt. And it ain't the thing to do, anyway. We're taking a murder charge with us that ought to be hung on someone else. And if you're a wise man, you'll let it rest there and forget about it. Savvy?"

Crosby nodded silently.

Lonesome caught the reins of Crosby's horse and rode hard away. Crosby stood, watching them go, silent, inscrutable.

"You ain't runnin' out with a murder charge hangin' over

us?" Tarnation stormed in disbelief. "Why didn't you make that buzzard come clean while we had him?"

"Wouldn't have done any good," said Lonesome. "There's just one chance, and I'm taking it. You'll have to bank on me, Tarnation."

"It's shore hard when you act like this," Tarnation snapped, but nevertheless he objected no more.

A mile from where they had left Crosby, Lonesome turned loose the led horse. They rode on, looking back constantly for some sign of pounding pursuit, but none appeared.

"Crosby's a smart man," Lonesome said finally. "I reckon he's decided to let well enough alone." He grinned to himself. "Too smart," he added, and did not amplify the remark when Tarnation looked at him inquiringly.

They rode leisurely for an hour, and Tarnation exclaimed suddenly: "You're bearin' off to the west!"

"That's right."

When the blazing sun ball was dropping fast to the far horizon and shadows were lengthening around them, Tarnation muttered: "Are you crazy? We're circling, right back to the Lazy H. Into more trouble."

"I was wondering if I had my bearings right." Lonesome chuckled.

"Crazy as a hydrophoby skunk!"

"I told you we had one chance," Lonesome said. "Either that or be runnin' from murder the rest of our lives. Not to speak of seeing that girl lose her ranch. Have you forgotten that sixty-eight hundred dollars her old man deposited?"

"Hell, no!" denied Tarnation profanely. "Ain't we charged with stealin' it? What's in your mind, Lonesome?"

Lonesome talked as they rode, and Tarnation's impatience vanished and a slow, grim smile came around his mouth. "It's a chance," he conceded. "I'm fur it."

51

VI

"DOUBLE SETTLEMENT"

Darkness was an hour old when Lonesome and Tarnation came in to the Lazy H Ranch from the south. There was no moon. The velvety blackness was like a sable cloak that hid all movement. The windows of the ranch house were little yellow squares of light, and they could see the bunkhouse lights beyond, also.

They rode boldly up the front of the house, dismounted, and went to the front door. The house was quiet, the hired hands back in the bunkhouse. There was no evidence of Crosby's men. Lonesome rapped on the door.

A moment later they heard quick, light steps answering the knock. The door opened, and the light behind framed a slender figure peering out to see who it was. Lonesome clapped a hand over her mouth just in time to cut off a scream. He swung her up in his arms.

"Don't you be afraid, miss," he hushed as he strode away from the *portal* with her. "I wouldn't hurt a hair of your head. We're just going to take a little ride."

She struggled wildly, but Lonesome held her firmly. It was an awkward job getting up on the saddle, but that was finally accomplished with Tarnation's help, and they rode quietly out of the yard and left the ranch house behind, unalarmed. For a mile Lonesome held his hand over his captive's mouth, reassuring her calmly. Finally she recognized the futility of struggling and lay quietly in his arms. When he judged they were out of earshot of the ranch, Lonesome took his hand away, saying apologetically: "I hated to do it this way, miss. But you were mighty stubborn this afternoon."

"Every man in the county will be after you with a rope when they know about this," she choked. "What are you going to do with me?"

"We're going to town."

"You're lying!"

"I reckon you know your directions," said Lonesome coolly.

She fell silent, her small body curled limply inside his arms. Warm and soft, Lonesome had never carried anyone like this before. It disturbed him somewhat.

"What are we going to town for?" she demanded suddenly.

"Just to annoy Crosby," Lonesome chuckled.

"I don't understand."

"I'd tell you," replied Lonesome, "but you wouldn't believe me. I'm going to show you with your own little eyes. You see, miss, you're about the only person Tarnation and I know we can trust around here."

"Trust? I . . . I hope they hang you both!"

Tarnation spat in the darkness alongside. "Wimmen can be the spitefullest critters I ever seen," he mused. "Look it the way the Indian squaws usta jump into the prisoners the bucks brought back."

"I'm not a squaw!"

"You're a woman," said Tarnation, as if that settled the question.

A little later, when the lights of Vallecito appeared briefly ahead of them as they topped a large rise, Leslyn Williams queried abruptly: "Who are you two men? I can't understand you, bringing me into town this way. You know what will happen to you."

Tarnation chuckled beside them. "We're just a coupla pore no-'count cowhands with a bad habit of ridin' around into trouble."

"You're outlaws."

"Looks like we are now," Tarnation agreed.

"I can't understand all this you are doing," she insisted stiffly.

"I don't reckon we do ourselves," Lonesome assured her. "Now there's Vallecito just ahead, miss. Will you give your promise not to scream when we get to the houses?"

"No!"

"Then I'll have to put my hand over your mouth again."

"Very well!" she stormed. "Anything to keep that filthy paw out of my face!"

"Thanks," said Lonesome gratefully. "I know I can trust you." And he didn't hear the startled little gasp she gave.

They rode into Vallecito, where the lighted adobe houses were thick on either hand, and their horses made little noise in the dry dust of the dark, narrow street. Only the plaza was lighted.

"Do you know where Bowers, the little bank cashier, lives?" Lonesome asked his prisoner.

"Yes," she sniffed.

"Show me," said Lonesome cheerfully.

Not many moments later they stopped before a house set back behind two cottonwoods and a picket fence. The front windows were lighted. Lonesome lowered his burden to the ground and climbed down beside her.

"Tarnation'll stay here with you," he said curtly, and left them there with the horses and strode to the house. His knock was answered by a short, buxom woman who looked at him challengingly.

Lonesome doffed his hat politely. "Is Mister Bowers in,

ma'am?" he queried.

"He is," she replied. "I'll get him." As she turned away from the door, her voice raised querulously: "Cyrus, someone at the door to see you."

Lonesome grinned to himself. The meek little Bowers had mated enthusiastically, if not wisely. A moment later the wizened figure of Bowers himself came to the door, peering through his spectacles.

"Howdy," said Lonesome briefly. "I got a little private business to talk over with you, mister."

Bowers recognized him with surprise, and stepped out, closing the door behind him. Lonesome's big hand clamped down on the wizened neck like a vise. His other hand jammed a gun muzzle into Bowers's side.

"Keep quiet, mister, if you value your health," he advised gruffly.

Bowers choked with surprise. He could hardly speak for a moment, and then he stuttered: "Wh-what d-does this mean? Wh-what are you d-doing with m-me?"

"Dragging you over to see your boss," said Lonesome curtly, and there was truth in the words for he had to half drag Bowers to the gate. "This little wart is going to take us over to Lemuel Stoddard's house," Lonesome said grimly to the two waiting there. "I reckon you'll want to go along peaceable now, miss?"

"I think you're losing your mind," she answered uncertainly.

"Doing without his likker allus effects him that way," Tarnation explained. "He gets violent when he ain't skin-full."

She ignored Tarnation pointedly.

As they started off, walking and leading the horses, Bowers bleated again: "I . . . I don't understand this, Miss Williams. I'll make trouble over this."

"You got all the trouble you can handle now," Lonesome assured him grimly. "Stoddard has laid a lot of dirty work on you to save his own skin."

Bowers gasped. "Stoddard! You mean . . . you mean . . . ?"

"You know what I mean," Lonesome growled. "About Henry Williams."

"But . . . but he couldn't do that. I haven't done anything!" Bowers protested almost tearfully.

"Stoddard says you did."

"He lies!" Shrill indignation replaced Bowers's fear. "He did everything! I've kept my mouth shut because he threatened me!"

"Threatened you with what?"

"I . . . I borrowed some money when he first took over the bank," Bowers confessed miserably. "He found it out, and since then he has held it over my head. But I didn't accept that deposit from your father, Miss Williams. Stoddard did that. And . . . and I didn't have anything to do with what followed. I didn't even know he was going to have your father killed." Bowers was almost sobbing now. "I'll tell," he gulped. "I've hated him day by day for three years while he cracked the whip over me."

"Money my father deposited?" Leslyn Williams whispered.

"Sixty-eight hundred dollars," Bowers babbled. "That day he was killed. I knew there was something wrong when Stoddard warned me to forget about it, and to say your father had not deposited any money that day."

"Who killed Williams?" Lonesome purred.

"I don't know," Bowers insisted. "Stoddard hurried out right away and was gone half an hour. And when he came back in, he was jumpy. I don't know who he saw."

"Who did you suspect?"

"I don't know," Bowers moaned. "Crosby came in all excited a few minutes after you left the bank. He talked with Stoddard privately and then hurried out. They've been working together for two years. Reaching out and swallowing off all the ranches around here, planning and scheming together. Crosby owns part of the bank stock secretly. I know that. This is where Stoddard lives."

"We'll go in and talk it over with Stoddard," Lonesome affirmed.

Lonesome tried Stoddard's door and found it unlocked. He opened it and walked in, and two men in the big room inside started to their feet. One of them, Stoddard, paled. The other, Crosby, spat out an oath and grabbed for the gun that had replaced the one he had lost to Tarnation and Lonesome.

Lonesome was taken by surprise, also. His gun barely came out as Crosby's did. For the second time that day he saw murder in Crosby's face. Their guns roared together, but Lonesome shot an instant sooner. He heard the dull smack of Crosby's bullet in the wall behind him as the big .45 flew from Crosby's hand and thudded on the floor. Cursing wildly, Crosby looked down at his bleeding wrist.

Tarnation charged past Bowers and Leslyn Williams, his gun out for action and his mustache bristling formidably. "Did he hit you, Lonesome?" he shouted.

"Nope," said Lonesome. "I out-lucked him. Better tie up his hand for him."

"Let the snake bleed to death!" Tarnation snorted as he walked over and picked up Crosby's gun. He shook it in Crosby's face. "Well, you skunk, we drawed to your card an' outplayed your hand."

Crosby's face was a livid mask. "What are you two doing back here?" he whispered harshly. His eyes slid uneasily to

Bowers and Leslyn Williams, standing by the door.

Stoddard was peering at Bowers, also. His round, pinkish face was pasty. His rimless eyeglasses had jerked awry when he jumped back from the shooting, and were still perched that way. He raised a shaking hand and adjusted them.

"Bowers!" he exploded. "Who asked you to come over here tonight?"

Bowers licked his lips and looked at Lonesome appealingly.

Lonesome grinned coldly. "Bowers has spilled the beans," he told Stoddard and Crosby. "You were pretty slick, Stoddard, when you tried to gobble that sixty-eight hundred dollars of Henry Williams's. His mortgage money, and there wouldn't be any left to meet the notes when you shoved them at his daughter. I reckon you thought that about clinched the Lazy H for you and Crosby, didn't you?"

"What sixty-eight hundred dollars?" Stoddard asked thickly. "I don't know what you're talking about."

"Bowers here says you do. He says you took it from Williams the day he was killed."

"He lies," said Stoddard flatly. "Where is the deposit slip? There was none found on the body. And Crosby was just telling me that, when his men searched you, there was no slip on you, although you had Williams's wallet and money."

"What were you two talking about a deposit slip for, before the matter was brought up?" Lonesome demanded shrewdly. "You hung yourself on a thorn then, Stoddard."

Stoddard glared at him. "We were just talking," he muttered.

"Well, anyway, without the deposit slip you figger there's no proof?" Lonesome asked mildly.

"I'll cheerfully go into court over it."

"I'll just save you the trouble," Lonesome told him. He

reached down to his belt and pulled out a heavy .45 cartridge. "It's wadded up inside here," he said calmly. "I figgered somebody might want it bad, and I better cache it where it couldn't be grabbed and tore up. All made out legal and plain to Henry Williams for six thousand, eight hundred, and fifty dollars, an' signed with your initials."

Stoddard suddenly looked sick, haggard.

"An' I'll just take it!" said a venomous voice at the end of the room, behind Lonesome and Tarnation. "Raise your fists, smart feller, an' chuck that ca'tridge over here."

Lonesome froze, then turned his head slowly. Parr, Crosby's foreman, was standing there with a gun in his hand, clad in trousers and a rumpled undershirt. Under the shirt a wide bandage covered his chest and left shoulder. Parr's hair was rumpled and his face unshaven. He had lost weight and looked weak and ill, but he was desperate now, the hate blazing in his eyes.

Lonesome's eyes narrowed. "Somebody shot you," he said.

Parr swore at him.

"Shot you from the front," Lonesome went on. "With a rifle, I bet. Parr, you're the sneak who bushwhacked Tarnation and me the day Crosby sent us out to his ranch. And you've been laying right here in Stoddard's house while you healed."

Parr did not try to deny it. "Heave that ca'tridge over here" he ordered again. "An' foller it with your guns. You an' that old wolf who runs with you."

"I been lookin' for you," Tarnation said grimly.

"Here I am," Parr sneered.

"Uhn-huh," Tarnation grunted. "I see you. Now . . . see me." As Tarnation spoke, he dodged aside and brought his big old-fashioned gun down, blasting as it came.

Parr shot him. Tarnation staggered, but the hammering roar of his shots did not break their rhythm. Parr went down in the doorway, still shooting wildly. Stoddard, cowering back against the wall, cried out in pain, went down to his knees, clutching his side.

"Parr hit me!" he sobbed. "He shot me! I'm dying!"

Tarnation swiftly thumbed fresh shells into his smoking gun. "I knowed I'd run across that curly wolf sometime an' get a shot at him," he said in a steady voice.

"You're hurt!" Lonesome exclaimed.

"Filed a little lead in my shoulder. Shucks, I'd had wuss an' never noticed it."

Feet pounded on the porch outside. Men burst into the room, led by a tall, stout man with a fierce mustache and a sheriff's star on his vest.

"What's goin' on in here?" the sheriff roared. "Put up them guns! The whole lot of you are under arrest! Who started this here war? My God, they're all half kilt!"

Stoddard was clutching his side and weaving weakly against the wall, moaning, slobbering with fear. "This is all your fault, Crosby," he sobbed. "I told you not to kill Williams. I knew. . . ."

"*Shut up, you fool!*" Crosby shouted.

But Stoddard was past heeding anything. This pale, pudgy man from outside the range country was beside himself with fear, the fear of lead and death. "I knew it was the wrong thing to try," he whimpered. "I said you'd better not kill him. And now look what's happened. I'm dying."

The sheriff listened with gaping jaw. "Killed Henry Williams?" he repeated stupidly.

"The man's out of his head!" Crosby snarled.

Leslyn Williams stepped to the sheriff's side. "You heard it," she charged. "Crosby shot my father, and Stoddard cov-

60

ered up a six-thousand-dollar deposit my father had made that morning. They thought they'd get the deposit slip and no one would know. They went after our ranch, like they've been after others in the valley here for two years . . . rustling, burning, shooting. Crosby and Stoddard were behind it all. Bowers told us."

"My gosh," the sheriff gasped, scratching his chin.

"She's right," Lonesome nodded. And swiftly he told what he and Tarnation had found the day they came to Vallecito and sketched in what had happened after that. "Lock us all up," he finished. "You can sort the truth out and put it down later."

"You won't lock these two up," Leslyn flashed, nodding at Lonesome and Tarnation. "They're the ones who brought the truth out this evening after Crosby tried to make it look like they killed my father."

The sheriff waved a hand helplessly at her. "All right. First off, I'll get the whole lot of you patched up so you won't die on me. An' you can stand good for these two men, Miss Williams. I guess, if you brought 'em into town once this evening, you can again. Come on, men, lend a hand here. Someone run for Doc Fletcher."

"I guess we better be going, soon as I get my shoulder patched up a little," Tarnation grumbled to Lonesome and Leslyn a few minutes later. "Too danged many questions around here."

"You'll stay in town and have that shoulder taken care of," Lonesome said flatly.

"An' what'll you do?"

"I'll take Miss Williams out to her ranch, if she wants me to," he said shamelessly. "She can ride your horse."

Leslyn's eyes were sparkling and a little moist as she

looked up at Lonesome's homely face. "I'm sorry for the things I said," she apologized breathlessly. "I didn't know."

"I've plumb forgot everything you said." Lonesome grinned.

"And I wish you would ride back with me," Leslyn pleaded. "It's a lonely road."

"Huh!" Tarnation snorted in disgust as they wandered to the edge of the porch together. "Wimmen!"

KILLER'S GUEST

This story was the seventeenth that T.T. Flynn completed in 1934. In the notebook where he kept track of his stories, their length, and the magazines to which they were sold and the titles under which they were published, Flynn noted that he had written 1,548 pages in 1934. It is perhaps worth remarking that he sold every story he wrote that year, as he did most years. Rogers Terrill at Popular Publications bought "Killer's Guest," as Flynn had titled this story, on September 15, 1934, and it appeared very shortly thereafter in *Dime Western* (11/15/34).

I

"BITTER HOMECOMING"

Dave Worth was coming home. The chains on his wrists and ankles rattled every time he moved on the hard wooden smoking-car seat. They had clanked all afternoon as the little narrow-gauge train worked its laborious way into the southeastern Colorado mountains, toward Lode City, where Dave Worth was going to be hanged.

Sam Dunn, the deputy sheriff, had been loudly confident when he locked the chains on Dave in Idaho. "I had these made to get him back safe," Sam Dunn had said to the Idaho sheriff. "He won't peel outta these."

The Idaho sheriff, fingering the reward check for two thousand dollars, had chuckled appreciatively. "Good idea," he had said. "He's costing you two thousand dollars. Be kinda hard to lose him."

"Hell and damnation . . . I won't lose him!" Sam Dunn had boasted.

Sam had kept his word. Within another hour the narrow-gauge train would crawl down from the steep precipices and black smoky tunnels into the valley where Lode City would be the end of the trail for Dave Worth. They would hustle Dave into jail and put an armed guard over him. They would try him solemnly before a jury of miners, cattlemen, and farmers, but the trial would be a farce. Dave Worth had been convicted when they had posted that two-thousand-dollar reward, for Lode City was going to hang Dave Worth for the murder of Colonel Henry Rittenhouse.

Dave again shifted his position on the hard wooden seat, and again the chains rattled. The fat man across the aisle turned his head and stared in fascination. Dave grinned at him. The fat man looked away hastily, uneasily. He knew—everyone in the smoker knew—why the prisoner was going to Lode City.

"Yep!" Sam Dunn had said loudly more than once to fellow passengers. "He's a bad one! A dirty drunk! Killed his friend. The colonel lent Dave twenty thousand to get a mine goin' . . . an', when the money was sunk in the ground an' all the colonel had was Dave's no-account notes, Dave up and kills the old man one night an' tried to set fire to the house. If a cloudburst hadn't come up, he might've got away with it, too. But the rain put the fire out. We found old Colonel Rittenhouse with his head beat in, four shots in his body, an' Dave's pipe on the table. The tracks of Dave's boots were still in the mud outside. To top it off the colonel had told some friends in the hotel he had to go home and meet Dave. We swore we'd get Dave for that. Slapped a two-thousand-dollar reward on him an' sent out notices. They picked him up in Idaho, an' now he's going back to hang."

Sam Dunn now sat there in the opposite seat, a big man, powerful, with an undershot jaw and a wide, loose mouth that could drink or talk with equal facility. He held one end of the lead chain in his hand. It ran to the leg iron between Dave's ankles, and up through a metal ring to the short chain binding Dave's wrists. A short hobbling step was all that Dave could make. A hard yank on the chain would double him up, pulling his wrists down to his ankles.

The train stopped a few minutes at a flag station, then rattled on, lurching, swaying, flanges shrieking on the sharp turns. Light from the brass lamps overhead glinted through the window at Dave's left, showing jagged walls of rocks. On the other side of the train the drops were steep and deep. Dave had been over this stretch many times. He could visualize each mile as plainly as if he were seeing them.

The rear door opened, admitting the conductor, who came to them, balancing expertly as he walked. He handed Sam Dunn a sealed envelope.

"Got this telegram for you when we stopped back there," the conductor said.

"For me! What in tarnation! We're 'most home now."

The conductor was thin, elderly, and his sharp, prying nose seemed to grow sharper as Sam Dunn read the message and whistled softly.

"Hell's to pay!" Sam growled. "They know we're comin', an' they're gatherin' by the station. This is from the sheriff. He tells me to get off at the flag station back there."

"Too late now," said the conductor.

Sam Dunn swore. "I don't want no lynchin'. I set out to bring this man home to jail, an' I aim to put him in there."

The conductor chewed reflectively. "I can't back the train up. There ain't a place to get off between here and Lode City. Sorry." He walked forward to the express car.

"Maybe the sheriff'll have some deputies to hold 'em back," Sam Dunn muttered.

Dave smiled thinly. He was lean, hard. From the moment of capture his face had shown few signs of emotion. Now he looked less worried than Sam Dunn. "That puts you up a tree, don't it, Sam?"

"It's liable to put you up a tree," Sam Dunn replied bluntly. "I'm tryin' to figger a way outta this."

Dave said calmly: "If the conductor won't back up, we're headed for Lode City in spite of hell 'n' high water. Build me a smoke, will you? If I'm going to swing, I might as well get used to it. Unlock one of my wrists. It'll be more comfortable."

"Can't," Sam Dunn groaned. "You know I mailed the key back to Lode City." He rolled a cigarette, put it between his prisoner's lips, lighted it. "You got a hangin' comin' to you sooner or later, anyway," he said callously.

"Maybe I didn't kill the colonel," Dave said.

"Hell, you're wastin' your breath. Too much proof against you."

"You dug it up, Sam. Why didn't you take time to dig up some proof I didn't do it?"

"You're guilty as hell," Sam Dunn said brusquely. "Take your medicine like a man."

"I reckon I'll have to," Dave agreed amiably. "Gimme another light on this."

Sam Dunn struck another match. Dave leaned forward, puffed, and then, as Sam tossed the match down, the prisoner's manacled wrists jammed violently into the other's unprotected stomach.

Sam Dunn emitted a mighty gasp. His body went lax. Eyes bulging, he heaved and gagged for his breath, half paralyzed. Dave Worth snatched the revolver and jumped into the aisle, chains rattling loudly.

The fat man cowed in his seat as Dave called loudly: "I'll kill the first man that moves!" He backed up the aisle with short, jerky steps.

The front door was only a few seats away. Chains rattling, the lead chain dragging on the floor, Dave backed toward it. The smile was gone from Dave's face. Grim, hard, threatening, he watched the passengers.

Sam Dunn staggered half up. "Stop him!" he bawled. "Somebody gimme a gun!"

"Sit down, Sam!"

The deputy looked at his former prisoner and sat down. "You can't make it," he warned loudly. "You jump with them chains an' it'll kill you!"

Dave's back touched the door. Whirling, he caught the doorknob with his free hand, jerked open the door, and lurched out on the rocking platform.

Back in the smoking car, a gun blasted loudly. A hole splintered in the door glass. Balancing on the uncertain footing, Dave looked back into the car and saw Sam Dunn, standing in the aisle with a revolver. Dave fired through the glass. Sam Dunn dove behind a seat. The other passengers were already down out of sight.

Dave grinned mirthlessly. Dust and cinders swirled across the platform. The rumble of the train's progress was loud against the rocky walls rising sheer on the inner side of the track. Off the other side of the platform was blank space. The cañon down here was a full two hundred feet deep. Explosives had blasted out this narrow winding ledge along which the roadbed ran.

Dave turned awkwardly again on the lurching platform. His ankles lacked freedom to step over to the express car. Gathering up the lead chain so that it would not drag, he jumped for the solid wooden door of the express car.

The revolver smacked hard against the express car door. Dave's other hand caught the door handle and twisted it. The door opened, precipitating him into the dim, cavernous interior.

The conductor and the shirt-sleeved express messenger were just ahead. They had heard the shot. The express man was lifting a shotgun off hooks above a little wall desk.

As he reeled to keep his balance, Dave yelled: "Get away from that!" He fired a shot into the ceiling for emphasis.

The express man stumbled back, lifting his hands. The conductor reached high and backed off.

"Has this train got those new-fangled air brakes?" Dave demanded.

"Y-yes," the conductor stuttered.

"Good. Then I know what you've got to do. Brakeman showed me one day. There's a valve under the back of this express car you gotta shut off before you pull the couplin' pin. Do that. I'll be squattin' in the doorway with this gun on you until she's cut. Don't try any foolishness!"

"I w-won't," the conductor stuttered.

Dave herded them to the rear door. The conductor and express man stepped over to the smoker platform. Dave crouched under possible gunfire from the smoking car, crouched and watched grimly while the conductor lay on his stomach, reached down between the two cars for the air cock. The strain on the couplings baffled him for a time, but slack came between the two cars, and he jerked the pin loose. The express car dropped back. An air hose parted with a loud *pop*. The rear section of the train slowed abruptly, vanished back down the track.

Dave closed and barred the express car door, hobbled quickly to the front of the car, and opened the door there. The light struck against the swaying engine tender. A narrow wooden sill ran along the base of the tender. At one corner a light iron ladder led to the top. Dave slipped the gun in his pocket. Risking another fall under the wheels, he jumped at the ladder, caught one side, hung on until his feet were secure, and awkwardly hauled himself up.

The fireman was bailing coal. The engineer was watching the water gauge and a roaring injector. Neither had noticed that most of the light train had been left behind. Dave waited until the fireman sat down, and dropped without warning into the cab.

His back against the coal gate, the gun in his hand, Dave motioned the fireman to him. "Get a hammer and chisel an' cut this chain between my legs."

The grimy young fireman obeyed quickly. From a bulkhead in the tank he took a heavy machinist's hammer, a big cold chisel, and a coal pick. Sitting down with the pick head across his knees, he went to work expertly with the hammer and chisel, using the pick head as a base. In a few minutes the chain between Dave's ankles parted.

Dave spread his legs and grinned. "That's better. Now I'll get on your seat. Put that pick on my lap an' cut the chain between my wrists."

It was risky. A bold man might have taken a chance with the hammer. But the fireman wasn't bold. The grizzled engineer watched in silence, gingerly working his throttle and brakes as the grade dropped steadily before them.

The wrist chain separated at one side. Dave had the

fireman cut through the other side, close to the cuff. That done, he stood up, ankles and wrists free, the hampering lead chain laying on the floor. He grinned at the fireman. "Never knew a little chain could make so much difference. How far is Lode City?"

The fireman looked out. "About seven miles."

"Roll up to the station an' stop," Dave said. "I'm goin' back up on the coal car. Got a gun . . . ? Never mind, lemme look."

Dave searched the fireman and engineer, found no weapons, and climbed back on the tank, ignoring the irons around wrists and ankles and the short ends of chain still attached to them.

He was standing on the tank top, cinders pelting against his face, when the engine and express car rolled into the valley and the winking lights of Lode City stood out ahead. In the distance he could see surging movement around the little wooden station. The sheriff's telegram had been right. A posse was gathering to meet Sam Dunn and his prisoner.

Dave quickly reëntered the express car and caught the shotgun off the wall hooks. A hunch made him lift the top of the desk. The express man's gun belt and .45 were inside. Dave hurriedly strapped them on, went to the rear door, opened it, and then dropped off into darkness.

He hit hard, floundering a moment—and then scrambled up a low bank and ran through a narrow patch of alfalfa, toward the first trees and scattered houses on the edge of Lode City.

The chain ends hanging from his wrists and ankles jingled faintly as he moved. Dave ignored them. He heard the train stop before the station, heard the low surge of many voices and excited yells, and, standing in the black shadows under an open front shed, he heard the rush of horsemen coming from the station, following back along the narrow-gauge railroad track.

The darkness hid a smile, grim, hard. Dave Worth had come home to Lode City, but there would be no hanging tonight. No hanging any time if he could have long enough to find the man whom Colonel Henry Rittenhouse had been expecting half an hour before the cloudburst—the man whom Dave Worth himself could not name.

II

"SCATTER-GUN CAPTIVE"

The Starbuck Mine was the biggest, on the north slope, a quarter of a mile above Lode City. Beyond was the Creole Girl and the Lucky Deuce, and scattered back in the rocky, forested cañons in a ten-mile radius were some properties still occasionally worked, and some that were idle or abandoned. Dave Worth's Kingpin Mine, whose vein had faulted, was one of these. The fruitless search for the lost vein had used up all of Colonel Rittenhouse's twenty thousand dollars.

Lode City was strung up and down the valley slope, small log and framed houses for the most part, tents on the outskirts, a brick building or so, including the courthouse on the short main street down by the station. Miners outnumbered everyone else in the Lode City bars, but there were cowmen from the lower valley and foothills to the south, prospectors, and a few businessmen.

Tonight men on foot filled the bars, milled along the main street. Lode City had been keyed for a hanging, and the excitement still hung in the air. Not a saddled horse or a rider was in sight on the main street. All riders and many men on foot had rushed up the railroad tracks to join in the hunt for the man they believed killed Colonel Henry Rittenhouse.

Many men knew Dave Worth by sight. Those who didn't could recognize him by the irons that Sam Dunn had locked on his wrists and ankles. Afoot, without food, water, he would not get far. There would be a hanging yet, men boasted.

Drifting through the dark side streets, Dave smiled thinly. Darkness was all that gave him life now. Every man's hand was against him. These people he had lived among, worked among, had turned alien. The shotgun cradled in his arm, the .45 at his belt, were all he could be certain of.

With that knowledge Dave walked with long, unhurried strides to the road that paralleled the main street. Here the houses were more numerous, more substantial. Several times men on foot appeared near him. But only the main street was lighted. Recognition was as difficult here as at the edge of town. Dave Worth was a condemned man, was already counted as good as dead. It gave him a curious feeling of detachment. Although there was no hope, he had no fear of what might happen. His stride was still unhurried as he cut through a vacant lot to the back of the buildings that fronted on the main street.

The Palace Hotel was two stories, frame construction, built like an L, with the bottom of the L facing the street. Lobby, bar, dining room filled the front, downstairs. The long shaft of the L was a two-story wing running back from the street. In the angle of the L was a hitch rack and place for buggies and wagons to stand. A buggy and two wagons were there now. Several horses were at the hitch rack. Two drunks were arguing at the end of the hitch rack as Dave walked into the yard. He had slipped his pants legs down over the ankle irons, pushed the wrist irons up as far as possible under his coat sleeves, but the chain ends of the ankles clinked softly with each step.

From the hitch rack, he heard a drunk talking loudly: " 'F I see 'im, I'll cut down on 'im an' kill 'im deader'n a mine timber! Where's m' horsh?"

" 'S wrong hoss, Jake."

"Nemmin'. He'll do."

They were still arguing as Dave opened the side door of the hotel, walked through a short passage, and came to the center hall of the long back wing. To the right the hall opened into the lobby, buzzing now with movement and conversation. To the left, in the back, were the rear stairs. Dave met no one, so he walked to the back and climbed to the second floor. The hall there was deserted. Several oil lamps in brackets cast an uncertain light. Dave walked to the front. The wooden floor creaked underfoot. The chain links on his ankles seemed to clink louder in the dim quiet.

A bearded miner stepped out of a room at the front of the hall, cast an incurious glance, saw the cradled shotgun, called jocosely: "Not lookin' for Dave Worth up here, are you?"

The man was a stranger. Dave chuckled. "He might be around here at that," he replied. "What does he look like?"

"Search me, stranger. Never saw him before, but I'll be there when they string him up. He's a low-down, ornery snake, from what I hear."

The bearded man's boots clumped down the front stairs, and the thin, expressionless smile came back to Dave Worth's face as he knocked on one of the room doors. Inside a voice called: "Who is it?"

"That you, Bartlett?"

"Yes," the voice answered impatiently, "just a minute."

73

Dave Worth opened the door and stepped in. "Take it easy, Bartlett," he said easily, closing the door. "I had an idea you'd be in here nursing a whisky bottle. Couldn't even leave it long enough to watch me hang, could you . . . ? Sit down an' keep quiet."

A brass lamp with a tin shade, on a writing table against the wall, threw light down on a big open ledger and a welter of papers. On the right side of the table were a quart whisky bottle and a pitcher of water. The man who stood in the center of the room had a glass in his hand.

A young man, no older than Dave Worth, he was thin, stooped, pale from lack of sunshine. His long hair was combed straight back. Weak eyes peered through steel-rimmed glasses. His nose was long, his face sharp. About him clung a furtive, rodent-like air as if, hidden from sun and light, he peered and burrowed at secret, furtive matters. Now the sharp face was a study in blank amazement, uneasiness, fear. The hand that held the glass began to tremble.

"Dave Worth," he said huskily.

"Uhn-huh. Dave Worth. Got some business with you, Bartlett."

"But . . . but they're looking for you," Bartlett babbled. "They're going to hang you. I was down at the bar a few minutes ago, and they were talking about it." Bartlett swallowed. A prominent Adam's apple in his throat bobbed up and down. "You . . . you'd better get out of here."

"Sit down, Bartlett. I'm safer here than anywhere else. Who'd think of looking for me in the hotel . . . or in the room of Colonel Rittenhouse's bookkeeper? They know you'd yell for the sheriff soon as you laid eyes on me. You would, wouldn't you, Bartlett, if you thought you could get away with it?"

"I don't want to see you, Worth. Get out. They . . . they'll think I'm hiding you. Maybe they'll string me up, too." The glass in Bartlett's hand trembled still more.

Dave grinned coldly, took a deep breath, shoved out his hands so that the wrist irons and chain ends showed.

"That'd make me laugh while they yanked me up in the air, Bartlett. I never had any use for you. The colonel kept you on the payroll because you could keep your nose in your books an' do the work better'n any man he'd ever hired. But he didn't like you, Bartlett. Set that glass down before you slop it."

Bartlett put the glass on the table. His eyes moved to the shotgun. He swallowed again. "Colonel Rittenhouse is dead. It doesn't matter now what he thought. I did his work and did it right."

"You're a liar, Bartlett. The night the colonel died he was worried. He'd been checking up. All day you worked at the mine office, and half the night you sat here in your room going over figures and swilling whisky. You never went anywhere. You didn't gamble or throw money away on women. You worked hard and saved half your salary. It was all there in the bank."

Bartlett said: "That's right. I'm steady. I . . . I drink a little, but it doesn't interfere with my work. I'm on the mine books tonight."

Dave Worth stared without blinking. His head was pushed slightly forward; his jaw was hard. "That's right," he admitted quietly. "But you're crooked, Bartlett. You look guilty as hell right now. The colonel had you nailed cold. For months you've been changing assay reports. Mighty near a hundred thousand in gold has been stolen since you were the kingpin. The colonel was ready to turn you over to the sheriff, but he wanted to find out first where the gold had gone."

Bartlett caught up the whisky bottle, tilted it, gulped. He

choked a little as he set it back. "You're making it up!" he gasped. "I never killed him. I was here at the hotel bar that night. I ate supper in the dining room, and went into the bar. I was there when they saw the fire. I can prove it."

"If you knew anything was going to happen, you'd be sure to fix an alibi. You're smart enough for that. The colonel was expecting someone that night. He told me he'd know before he went to bed just what he was going to do about it. A man was coming who owed him money and who could help him out on it."

"I don't know anything about it," Bartlett said. He spoke with an effort. His hand shook as he passed a handkerchief over his face.

Dave said: "They're hunting me tonight. They'll riddle me with lead, or hang me if they can. I can't waste time on your lies. You kept the colonel's private books. Where are they?"

Heavy steps came along the hall outside. Bartlett's eyes went to the door. He hesitated. The thought in his mind was plain.

"One yip out of you and I'll turn loose with this scatter-gun," Dave warned softly. "Where are the colonel's books? At the mine office?"

"Yes," Bartlett nodded. Through the glasses an idea gleamed in his weak eyes.

Dave's face hardened. "Shouldn't be anyone in the mine office right now. But maybe there is. Maybe you figure it's a neat trap. If it is . . . I'll kill you first, Bartlett. Ready to chance it?"

"Wait!" Bartlett begged. He gulped from the bottle again, choked again, wiped his mouth with the back of his hand. "I forgot," he muttered. "The colonel's daughter took his records. She's got 'em at the house."

"Daughter? What daughter? I never knew he had a daughter."

"She was back East," Bartlett said. "She took the first train out here. Been here a week. Gloria Rittenhouse is her name. She took all his papers to the house. She's staying there with some woman relative who came out here with her."

"Then we'll go to the house," Dave decided curtly. "Get your hat and come along."

Bartlett's voice cracked. "They'll shoot me, or hang me if they catch me with you. Let me stay here. I'll keep quiet about you."

"Bartlett, I don't trust you half as far as a prairie rattler. Come quiet and peaceful because I'm jumpy tonight. I want to get you to the colonel's daughter alive."

III
"YELLOW DOG'S CHANCE"

Gray-faced, Bartlett sidled along the upper hall. He stumbled once as they started down the back stairs. Dave caught him by the shoulder, steadied him. "Keep ahead of me," he ordered. "No tellin' who'll look back from the lobby and recognize me."

Bartlett's movements were jerky and wooden as they walked half the length of the lower hall and turned right through the short passage to the side door. It opened before they got there. A lanky cowman wearing a black Stetson tramped in noisily. He cast an indifferent look at them, stiffened with recognition.

"Dave Worth," he rasped, and snatched for the gun on his hip. The next moment his hands shot in the air. His eyes glued on the shotgun muzzle that had poked past Bartlett's shrinking shoulder. "You got me," he said harshly. "Gonna kill me, I suppose."

"Maybe, Trompet. Turn around and I'll take your gun. . . . That's better. Now haul down your hands and walk outside easy with Bartlett here. You were fixing to take me, weren't you?"

"You're darn tootin'," Trompet admitted bluntly as he stepped outside. "They're looking fer you out in the hills, Worth. What're you doin' here in town?"

"Paying visits, Trompet. Easy with your tongue. One of these wagons yours?"

"Nope. Rode in."

"This nearest wagon'll do, anyway. Climb on the seat, both of you. I'll ride the bed behind. Drive out the back way, up toward the colonel's house."

Dave spoke under his breath. The two drunks were still arguing over by the hitch rack. They stopped as Trompet took the reins and swung the team of horses around. One of them said loudly: "That feller jus' rode up. Wha' he doin' on that wagon?"

"Nemmine. Which hoss you gonna take?"

The wagon clattered out of the yard. The hotel dropped behind. They turned away from the main street, turned again down a dark side road, drove toward the north of town at a smart trot.

Trompet spoke over his shoulder: "You can't get away, Worth. Every trail outta these parts'll be watched."

"Keep driving, Trompet."

"I've got a family," the cowman said desperately. "Gimme a chance, will you?"

"I've got a neck, Trompet. Who's giving me a chance for that?"

"You killed a man in cold blood. It's between you an' the law."

"Lynch law now, Trompet. I'm making my own law. Keep quiet when you pass these men ahead."

Two horsemen were closing in through the dim moonlight. Dave crouched in the jolting wagon bed, lowering the shotgun as they passed. He saw the men look hard at the wagon, saw them turn in their saddles and stare after it. Wondered why they did it, and put them out of his mind as the men rode on into town.

Colonel Rittenhouse had built his house midway between town and his mine. It stood on a little rise of ground, next to the road, with pine trees behind it. Of frame construction with a long wooden porch and white pillars in front, it was a modest place for the owner of the Starbuck Mine. But Colonel Rittenhouse had lived alone when he was in Lode City, lived simply, eating at the hotel, having a woman in on certain days to tidy the house, driving a buggy from the livery stable.

The front yard was deserted. The house windows were lighted. Trompet's voice sounded queer as he brought the wagon to a stop. "What are you fixin' to do, Worth?"

"Pay a visit. Get in the house."

Dave jumped to the ground, waited with the shotgun. His two prisoners climbed down, went to the porch ahead of him. The wagon's arrival had been noted. As they stepped on the porch, a woman opened the door, peered out. She was a young woman. Another woman stood behind her shoulder.

The young woman in the doorway said uncertainly: "What is it, Bartlett?"

Dave spoke past them. "We've come on a little business, miss. We'll have to come in."

His sidestep brought him into the light. She saw him clearly for the first time. A puzzled frown crossed her forehead. She said: "I don't believe I know you. Who are these gentlemen, Bartlett?"

She was tall, slender, dressed in black mourning. Young, too, despite the sober, mature black. Her features were delicate, clean-cut, and yet having a bit of the colonel's kindly force about them.

Bartlett cleared his throat, more uncertain than she. Dave spoke for him. "Get in, boys. Sorry, miss, but we'll have to come in."

Her look at him was level, estimating. She stepped back inside. "Come in the parlor," she said.

Her companion was a stoutish woman in her fifties, unfriendly, suspicious, nervous now. Her lips pressed tightly as Dave walked after Bartlett and Trompet with the shotgun muzzle covering their backs.

"Is it necessary to bring in a gun like this?" she said with asperity as Dave passed her.

"It's quite all right, Minnie, if he feels he must bring it in," Gloria Rittenhouse said calmly.

Dave smiled at her as the two women followed them into the parlor.

"Thank you, miss," he said. "Seems like I can't bear to let my hands off this gun tonight. Bartlett and Trompet here understand how it is, don't you, boys?"

Bartlett's Adam's apple moved as he swallowed. His sharp, furtive face looked haunted. Trompet spoke harshly: "Yes, please understand, Miss Rittenhouse, this man is. . . ."

"Never mind, Trompet. "I'm Dave Worth, miss."

"Dave Worth?" She was puzzled, did not place him. Then, with a rising note of disbelief—"Dave Worth. The man who . . . ?"

"I didn't do it, miss."

The stoutish lady said faintly: "Gloria, this isn't the man

who murdered your father . . . they said he had been captured in Idaho some place."

Gloria Rittenhouse ignored her. Her eyes were still wide. "They're bringing Dave Worth back on the train tonight. In chains. The sheriff told me. They did catch him in Idaho."

Dave shoved out his wrists. The irons, the chain links, stood out boldly against his skin. "They're looking for me now. The sheriff and the whole town. They aim to lynch me tonight."

Gloria Rittenhouse hardly took her eyes from Dave. Color had surged into her cheeks. Her slender hands were clenched. "I don't know what happened," she gasped. "I hope they get you quickly and hang you. How dare you come here to this house? If I were a man . . . if I had a gun. . . ."

"I'd feel the same way you do, if I thought what you do. And everyone thinks the same," Dave said bitterly. "But I didn't do it. Your father was my friend."

"And you killed him?" More bitter than he, she lashed him with the accusation.

"I didn't. I'm trying to prove I didn't."

"Why are you here with these men?"

Dave Worth could still grin although it held little humor. "I brought Bartlett because he's a snake. He cleaned the Starbuck Mine of over a hundred thousand in gold. He knows that I know it now. Trompet's here because he's all man, and would help hang me because of your father. They're the only ones who know where I am."

"I know where you are. I'll get word to the sheriff as fast as I can. You won't shoot me in front of these people. You kill in secret and run. You're a coward."

She started toward the door. Dave stepped over, blocked her way. "Of course, I won't hurt you, miss. But maybe your wildness will put ideas in Trompet's or Bartlett's head. I might have to shoot them."

Trompet spoke grimly: "He'd do it, if he thought he had to, Miss Rittenhouse. I guess I'd do the same in his place. He's on the run from a rope, an' he ain't no coward. I never could figure how come he shot your father. That wasn't Dave Worth's style. Maybe you'd better listen to him."

Eyes blazing, she stepped back. "What is it you want here?"

The East hadn't made her much different from her father. She thought straight, acted without hesitation. In danger she was prettier than ever.

"You've got your father's books," he said. "His private books. The ones with his loans entered in them. I want to see them."

"Why?"

"Because," said Dave, "I'm trying to save my neck. Did you ever wonder how it'd feel to swing in a noose for something you didn't do? Ever wonder how it'd feel to come back in chains to a mob that was waiting to lynch you before you had a chance to tell your side?"

"Mob?"

"They were waiting at the station." Dave looked at the irons on his wrists. "I got rid of the chains . . . jumped off the train before it got in. I'm working fast before they catch up with me."

"Were they going to lynch him?" she asked Trompet.

"I reckon so. Nobody's got much use for him now."

She stared at Dave for a long moment. "I'll get the books," she said abruptly. "I'd give even a mad dog that much chance. But I can't see what connection my father's books have with this matter."

"Maybe none," said Dave. "Maybe a lot. When you're

dodging a noose, you grab at any bet. I'm playing out a hunch on this."

She walked out of the room with no further assurance that she would return, and was back in a few moments with several small ledgers. She put them on the table.

"I want to know what loans were due three weeks ago . . . the week your father was killed," Dave said. "They're entered. The colonel put everything down."

"Yes. I saw the item about a large sum you owed him," Gloria Rittenhouse said coldly.

"Due in six months, miss. He extended it that last night I called to see him. We decided there wasn't any use in sinking more money in my mine. It was closed up, done, finished. I owed the colonel twenty thousand. He knew he'd get it someday. There wasn't twenty thousand around Lode City for me to raise it. I had a friend up in Idaho who was scratching out what looked like a good proposition on some claims he'd staked. I headed toward him that night. Rode my horse a week through the mountains for a little change and fun. Got to my friend . . . and the first time we came into town the sheriff nabbed me."

She was looking through one of the ledgers.

"It was six months," she admitted. "An entry was made . . . extending it. I'm wondering if he made that last entry at the point of a gun? Here is the page, and here on the next two pages are listed personal loans and when they were due. I looked at them the other day. That week. . . ."

"Wait!" Dave said. "Don't read it out loud. I'd rather only us two know."

She made no protest as Dave stepped to the table and, keeping an eye on his prisoners, glanced at the ledger pages. He flipped the small ledger shut.

"Thanks, that's all I wanted to know," he said. "I've got an idea who killed your father now. Hold all this, please. I may be wanting it in court."

She studied him with no expression on her face. "I think you are going to hang," she told him evenly. "But if these accounts are ever needed in court, they'll be there."

She went out of the room with the ledgers.

Bartlett shifted uneasily. "You can't tie me into this trouble," he said defiantly. "If I got any gold, what'd I do with it?"

Dave smiled coldly at him. "I wonder," he said.

Trompet cleared his throat. "What're you fixin' to do now, Worth?"

"Keep my neck out of a noose. Hate to have to take you two along. You're in my way, but I can't let you get the posse after me."

Window glass crashed at the side of the room. A voice yelled: "Stick 'em up, Worth! You're covered!"

Dave's back was to the window. He saw the look of relief on Trompet's face, the quick triumph on Bartlett's as he swung the muzzle of the shotgun slightly. The blast of its shot rocked the whole room—and the lamp shade and chimney on the center table dissolved in fragments, plunging the room into blackness.

IV

"DEAD MAN'S STORY"

A second shot dinned against the roaring reverberations of the shotgun charge as Dave hurled himself across the room. He felt the hot crease of a bullet along his hip, and then he was through a door in the rear of the room into the darkness of the next room, heading for the rear of the house.

No lamps were lighted in the back. In the darkness he collided with Gloria Rittenhouse. Her cry of dismay was tinged with fright this time. Dave steadied her in the darkness.

"The law's outside! I'm leaving, miss. If I don't make it, think a little better of me. You heard the truth tonight."

Dave left her there, headed for the back door. She could have called a warning. She didn't. . . .

He left the shotgun on the kitchen floor, opened the rear door quickly, silently, and lunged out into the night with a .45 in his hand. He didn't know how many men were out here in the night, how they had found him, but if they bottled him in the house, there would be no chance to get away.

A man ran around the corner of the house, saw Dave coming out, and blazed at him with a six-gun.

He missed. Dave's answering shot found some part of its target, for the man lurched, plunged back around the house corner out of sight. Dave could have shot him again and did not. He wanted no killings on his hands. Voices were shouting out front as Dave raced for the pine trees just behind the house.

They had thought him bottled up in the parlor, hadn't put a guard back here. He crashed into the screen of bushes that had grown up at the edge of the trees. Guns were barking at the back corner of the house; lead was singing around him as he vanished from sight.

Men back at the house were shouting. They'd be in saddles in a moment. The shots would be heard far and wide. The pack would begin to close in on the spot from all points. The hunt was on in full cry now.

Beyond the bushes, the pine trees stood thickly in blackness. Occasional thin shafts of moonlight helped vision none at all. The thick carpet of needles crunched softly underfoot. Half a mile or so beyond lay the foothills. He might get to them, lose himself for the night, but with daylight they would be combing the whole area. They'd get him.

If he could stay near town, there might be a chance yet. Dave turned sharply to the right, ducking, dodging trees, low branches. He was still going when horsemen crashed through the bushes well behind him.

They paused for a moment, searching the spot where he had vanished, evidently hoping a shot had brought him down, and then spread out, working back and forth toward the foothills.

The trees formed a big semicircle about the rise of ground on which the house stood, running down nearer the road on the south and north sides. Dave made his way through them on the south side until he was opposite the house. Parting branches, he looked toward the house. Lamps had been lighted again. Figures were moving back and forth.

Several saddled horses were standing in front of the house. The wagon was still there. Dave slipped toward the house, watching for a challenge as he drew near, but none came. The riders of these horses were inside.

As he came up to the house, the front door opened. A man stepped out, listened a moment, called back in the house: "I won't hafta ride in for the posse. I hear 'em comin' now. I'll ride out an' meet 'em."

Dave heard it, too—the distant drum of galloping hoofs on the hard-packed road. More men were coming fast. He stepped behind the nearest horse as the speaker walked off the porch, spurs jingling. The man came to the horses, caught a pair of reins, turned the stirrup. His hearing was acute, for he caught the faint crunch of Dave's steps behind him. Dropping the stirrup, he turned quickly.

The barrel of Dave's gun caught him behind the ear, and he dropped without a sound. Dave holstered the gun, clapped the man's big hat on his own head, heaved the limp form off the ground, carried it hurriedly toward the corner of the porch. Through the open door he glimpsed another man talking in the parlor doorway, heard the words: "I knowed something was wrong about that wagon when we passed it, Trompet. I saw Ben Edwards drive in town this afternoon with them paint ponies. He had no business out toward the mines. When we got to the hotel an' heard the wagon had been stolen, the bunch of us rode out to have a look-see."

Dave rolled his burden under the edge of the porch out of sight and returned to the horses. He was swinging into the saddle when the speaker stepped on the porch and called to him.

"We'll wait here for the boys, Slim."

"Yep," Dave said over his shoulder as he headed toward the road.

His first impulse had been to get on a horse and ride away. Now another idea banished that. He waited by the side of the road until the vanguard of the posse galloped up.

One of the leaders called: "Where's the shootin' out here? Anybody get track of Dave Worth?"

"Found him in the house, there," Dave said rapidly, keeping his head down so the hat brim shadowed his face. "He shot the light out, got out the back door, and ran into the trees. Some of the boys are following him."

An incredulous oath greeted that. A rider spurred to the front.

"Get after him, then!" Sam Dunn ordered savagely. "He can't get far on foot. I'll find out what he was doing here. Spread out an' try to head him off before he gets out of those pines. Remember he's armed. Plug him on sight!"

They turned off the road in a surging wave and swept back toward the trees. Sam Dunn galloped to the house. Dave rode slowly after him.

The deputy sheriff swung to the ground and hurried into the house. Dave urged the horse quietly to the broken parlor window, any noise he made being drowned out by new members of the posse galloping past.

He heard Sam Dunn asking gruffly: "What was Worth doing here, miss? Did he bother you? I'm the deputy sheriff."

"He came here for some information," Gloria Rittenhouse replied. "He was polite enough about it. What will your men do if they catch him?"

"Shoot him," Sam Dunn said angrily.

"But he says he didn't kill my father. Is . . . is there a chance he's right?"

"No more chance than if I did it," Sam Dunn assured her. "He'll try to lie out of it, of course. But we'll get him. What did he want?"

Bartlett's high voice broke in: "He wanted to see what loans were due that week. Worth claims another man was coming to see Colonel Rittenhouse later that night, and that man killed the colonel, and he seems to think he can prove it. He showed up at my hotel room to make me take him to the mine office where the books were. When I told him they were here, he made me come with him so I couldn't give an alarm. This man recognized him, and Worth threw a gun on him, too."

"You're a fool, Bartlett!" Sam Dunn said angrily. "Why didn't you lead him to the mine office?"

Bartlett answered sullenly: "He said he'd kill me if anything happened there. I wasn't taking any chances."

"Do anything to save that hide of yours, wouldn't you, Bartlett? What did Worth think he was going to do?"

"I don't know," Bartlett answered.

Trompet continued: "That's what's worryin' me. What did Worth take all this chance for if he didn't think he was right? He could've kept goin'. Instead, he stops and fools around here."

"Won't do any good, anyway," Sam Dunn snorted. "The boys are on his heels."

Gloria Rittenhouse said: "You talk as if it didn't make any difference, whether he is guilty of not. If he killed my father, I want him to hang for it. But if he didn't, he should have a chance to prove it."

"Yes, miss." But Sam Dunn's agreement was merely perfunctory.

"Furthermore, I want you to arrest Bartlett," Gloria said evenly. "Dave Worth accuses him of stealing gold from the Starbuck Mine."

"He lied," Bartlett said violently. "There's no proof of anything like that!"

Sam Dunn protested. "He's your bookkeeper, Miss Rittenhouse. Worth'd lie about anything now. Bartlett seemed to satisfy your father."

"He didn't," she said calmly. "A week before my father died he wrote me that large sums had been stolen from the mine and he suspected his bookkeeper of having a major part in it. I have been having Bartlett watched and checked since I've been here."

"You mean, Miss Rittenhouse, you've got proof that Bartlett has been stealin' gold?"

"Yes. He continued to do it, evidently thinking it was safer after my father was gone. I will make the charge against him."

Bartlett's voice rose in desperation. "You can't put me in jail on talk."

"I not only can . . . but I will, Bartlett. I'll see the sheriff about you in the morning."

Outside the window Dave Worth smiled grimly as Trompet said slowly: "Where were you the night Colonel Rittenhouse was killed, Bartlett?"

"In the hotel bar," Bartlett said shakily. "I can prove it."

Sam Dunn said gruffly: "If you can prove it, you don't have to worry about it. I reckon I'll have to arrest you, Bartlett. But I ain't got time to take you in. I've got to get out after Dave Worth. Trompet, I'll make you a deputy an' you can take him to jail . . . unless you'd rather have one of the other men do it."

"I'll do it," Trompet agreed. "Gimme a pair of handcuffs. I don't want him divin' off the wagon seat while I'm rasslin' with the reins."

"You can't do this to me!" Bartlett protested wildly. "Why . . . why. . . ."

"Shut up!" Sam Dunn barked. "If Miss Rittenhouse is makin' a charge against you, I got to send you to jail. Maybe you'll be out pretty quick. It'll take a heap of provin', unless you turn out a weak fool an' admit a heap of things you say you didn't do."

One of the other men who had been quietly standing in the room chuckled and said: "You'll admit 'most anything, if they take a whisky bottle away from you long enough, Bartlett."

"I'll warn the sheriff not to let him have any," Gloria Rittenhouse said crisply.

"Gimme the handcuffs," Trompet requested. "Any you boys ridin' into town?"

"We'll all ride after the others," Sam Dunn said. "Need everybody we can get. Let's go, men. Worth hasn't run far."

Dave rode quietly over to the trees, barely reaching them before the men hurried out of the house, mounted, spurred off toward the foothills. Their crashing progress was receding back to the trees when Trompet put his prisoner in the wagon and drove off. Once the wagon had gone a short distance, Dave rode after it.

He caught it a quarter of a mile down the road, paced the wagon on Trompet's side. The rancher slowed the horses to a walk and peered over at him, then yanked on the reins, leaning out, staring. In the sudden quiet around the motionless wagon his voice was stunned: "Dave Worth!" Then: "Where'd you get that hoss an' hat?"

"Visiting around," said Dave. "You're a square shooter, Trompet. I need your help. Men'll believe what you say. Bartlett here knows where that stolen gold went. He knew something was going to happen to the colonel that night, for he made an alibi for himself. The colonel was killed because of that stolen gold, but that's not the only way Bartlett would be hooked up with it. He knows who killed the colonel. I aim to get the truth out of him before he shows up at the jail. I know now, but I can't prove it. His word'll clinch it. An' if we can pin that stolen gold on the other party, it'll clinch it twice."

"I don't know anything about it," Bartlett denied vigorously. "Let 'em put me in jail. I won't be there long."

"You will with Miss Rittenhouse pressin' a charge against you," Trompet assured him curtly. "I'm goin' to turn you over to the sheriff myself. What Worth says makes sense to me. I aim to be square about this. If you know anything that'll help him, he's goin' to get it here. Last chance he'll have, I guess. He won't be able to get at you in jail. I can't stop him, anyway. I ain't got a gun."

A dead stick snapped over in the trees lining the road. Dave looked warily at the spot, listened, but no more sounds came.

"I'm jumpy tonight," he confessed. "Get down out of that

wagon, Bartlett. You're going to talk, if I have to leave you dead in the road here."

"Wh-what are you gonna do?" Bartlett stammered. "Trompet . . . I'm a prisoner. Handcuffed. You're supposed to take me to jail."

"I can't help you," Trompet shrugged. "Better tell him what you know."

Bartlett stood up slowly, unwillingly, and turned to step over the wheel to the ground. The peace about them was broken by the sharp report of a rifle close by. Dave heard the sodden impact of the bullet, heard Bartlett's cry of fear, and the man pitched limply to the ground.

V

"KILLER'S GOLD"

Dave was swinging out of the saddle as Bartlett started to fall. He heard the boards in the wagon bed clatter as Trompet threw himself back into the slight cover that the low wagon side afforded. The gunman was in the trees just ahead, close by the side of the road. The stick had cracked at about the same spot. Dave put two shots there—waited in the shelter of his horse. The wagon team fidgeted nervously but stood still. No more shots came.

Trompet raised his head. "Wonder if you got him." A moment later Trompet, listening, said: "Nope. There he goes on a hoss back in there." Trompet stood up, jumped out of the wagon. "I wonder who'n hell did that! Hit Bartlett square! Couldn't 'a' been one of the posse mistakin' him for you."

"No," said Dave. "Whoever was there heard us talking. He knew who Bartlett was. An' if he hadn't intended to plug Bartlett, he'd have come out here and made himself known. He tried to get me, too. Trompet, that man wanted Bartlett dead. And the only man tonight who'd want him dead is the man who killed Colonel Rittenhouse. He was afraid Bartlett was going to talk, so he killed him."

"Not quite," said Trompet as the form over which they were bending stirred, groaned. Bartlett was conscious.

They had to lean close to hear him. Trompet struck a match. Bloody flecks were on Bartlett's lips. He choked. His breathing was becoming harder, more labored each moment. A little blood marked the hole in the front of his shirt, but not much.

Dave said grimly: "He won't last but a few minutes. Bartlett, you understand that?"

Between spasms of choking, Bartlett signified that he did. Dave raised Bartlett's head and shoulders. "Where's the gold, Bartlett?" he pleaded. "It won't do you any good now. You know who shot you. So do I. But he'll go free unless we find him with the gold."

Bartlett stiffened, fought to clear his throat. "Didn't know . . . he'd do it," he got out in words barely audible. "Gold's in mine office . . . behind board in back wall, right corner. He's only . . . only other one knows where. . . ."

"What's his name?" Trompet urged.

Bartlett's whole frame shook with a choking spasm—he gasped, gagged as Dave tried to lift him higher, and ease him. Then, abruptly, he was limp, quiet.

"That bullet did what it was aimed to do," Dave said, "stopped Bartlett from giving any names. But he said enough. We know where the gold is. And Bartlett said only one other man knows the spot. That's the man who killed him. If he shows up there after the gold, we've got him cold."

Trompet regarded him a moment. "But you'll hang anyway if you're around here long. Those shots'll draw plenty men."

"Are you telling me to escape, Trompet?"

Trompet cleared his throat. "I ain't got a gun," he pointed out sheepishly. "I got to do as you say, Worth. But if I was you an' had any sense, I'd get up to the mine office an' see about that gold. An' take a witness along."

Dave chuckled easily. "Trompet, you're a man. You took the words out of my mouth. I'm sticking a gun under your nose and telling you to come along. Leave the wagon here. You can climb on the horse in back of me."

Riding double, they left the spot, turning back up the road toward the Starbuck Mine. When they had gone a little way and heard riders crashing through the trees toward the road, Dave reined off on the other side into cover and went on through the trees. Trompet could have reached his gun in Dave's belt, if he'd wished. He did not appear to think of it.

"Didja kill the guy this hoss belonged to?" Trompet asked.

"Nope. I'm not a killer, Trompet. I had to gun-whip him, but I reckon he'll come around all right. He's hid under the Rittenhouse porch."

"Good," said Trompet. "You'd've been in as bad a pickle as ever if you'd plugged him. Who's this pardner of Bartlett's you say you've spotted?"

"Wouldn't do any good to tell you now."

They came to the mine through trees that studded the mountain slope. Ahead of them the mine lights winked in the night. The steady roar of the stamps grew louder. Deep in the mountain men were toiling in little black tunnels, and on the surface activity seethed without end. Distant gunshots could hardly be heard.

The mill straggled up the side of the mountain toward the shaft head, a long, huge building that went up and up, and vomited the ceaseless roar of machinery. At the bottom, in a wing that jutted off to one side, was the mine office that in daylight seethed with activity, also, and that at night was more or less deserted. The shadows were thick around it now and the windows were dark as Dave left the horse back up on the hillside and walked forward with Trompet. For all of the activity about the mine, no men were in sight at the moment.

"Don't look like any gold is hid around here," Trompet said, raising his voice above the cacophony of mine machinery. "Now I can't figure a stranger ridin' up here to get anything out of the office. Too likely to be seen. How much gold was gone?"

"Over a hundred thousand."

"Hell! How much'd that weigh?"

Dave thought a moment. "Over three hundred pounds. One horse could carry it. Gold bars wouldn't take up much space. Here's how I figure. With Bartlett gone, he'd want to get the gold quick. No use leaving it hidden any more. The game's up, finished. No better time to get it than tonight. Soon as Bartlett's death gets out, there'll be plenty watching and looking for the gold. Somebody'll be sure to wonder about the mine office and look around. I suppose it was hidden there in the first place because that was nearest and easiest, and Bartlett was there all the time to keep an eye on it."

"Sounds good, anyway," Trompet admitted. "Hell, who's this?"

A man stepped out of the darkness behind the office, holding a shotgun. He stared from under the brim of a black slouch hat as he came closer.

"What're they doin' about Dave Worth?" he called.

Dave dipped his head so the brim of the big hat hid his own face. "Still lookin' for him," he said. "Who are you?"

"Night watchman around here. Didn't know but what Worth 'ud show up here. I been waitin' around."

"Know him?"

"I've seen him," the watchman replied.

Dave said: "They're trying hard enough. Anybody ride up here in the last quarter of an hour and go in the office there?"

"Nary a soul. I've been standing here that long. Nobody been in the office since the night shift went on. The checkers have got their own office up by the shaft head. This office is locked. Say, mister, you remind me a lot of Dave Worth. Lemme see your face."

"Sure," said Dave Worth obligingly. "I'll take your gun first." He caught the shotgun with one hand, pushed a six-gun in the watchman's ribs with the other.

"Hell 'n' damnation!" said the watchman. "I'll get fired for this. You ain't goin' to plug me, are you, Worth?"

"Not if you keep quiet, mister. Any more watchmen around here?"

"Nary a one. That gun's hurtin' my ribs."

"Good thing you aren't ticklish," Dave said. "Both of you get back there against the building where it's dark."

"We're goin'," said Trompet hastily. "Just go easy with that gun."

Trompet was docile. The watchman was docile. Dave stood behind them with the shotgun in one hand and the belt gun in the other. Minutes passed. The roar of the mill was unending.

Trompet turned his head, spoke near Dave's ear. "Man ridin' down the slope. Caught a snatch of him in the moonlight up there."

"Keep quiet," Dave warned the watchman.

96

They shrank back to the shadows. Down from the trees and the shadows and patches of thin moonlight on the mountain slope came a lone horseman, riding slowly. He seemed to be watching on all sides as he came, but the shadows were black behind the mine office. The three men there stood motionless. The watchman seemed to be catching on. The rider came almost to them, dismounted, walked hurriedly around the building corner to the front.

Trompet put his mouth close to Dave's ear and said: "That the man?"

"Uhn-huh."

"My God. Gimme my gun. I know *who* that is."

Dave returned Trompet's .45. "He ought to be inside now, if he's going. Let's see."

Pushing the watchman ahead, Dave led the way cautiously around the building. The rider was not in sight in front. The office door was closed.

Through one of the windows a match flared for a moment at the back of the office, was hastily shielded.

"Right hand corner, at the back," Trompet said. "Want me to go in?"

"I'll go in," Dave said. "He won't take this lying down. You two men can back me up."

Trompet nodded agreement. The watchman seemed willing to play along. His shotgun was returned. Dave waited a moment, then gun in hand walked up the office steps on his toes, tried the door knob softly. It was open. He hurled the door back and lunged in. "Get away from that gold!" he called into the darkness. "And come out with your hands up!"

Silence for a moment. A long counter ran around the middle of the room. Beyond it there was no movement. Trompet and the watchman came in through the doorway.

"Where is he?" the watchman asked.

From the blackness at the back of the room an orange streak of flame lighted the crash of a shot. Dave's right shoulder numbed as a bullet smashed into it. He staggered, raising his gun with the other hand. He heard the watchman yell and tumble back out of the doorway. Another shot blasted from the back of the room. A window crashed out back there as Dave shot awkwardly with his left hand. Beside him Trompet's big .45 thundered at the same moment. They had both jumped forward in a crouch, shot over the top of the counter.

No other shots were fired back at them. Trompet's voice rasped on the silence. "He's got out that window!"

There was no answer to that.

"I'll see," Dave grunted.

His shoulder was beginning to hurt. He could feel the blood running down his arm. He ignored it as he walked around the end of the counter, back through the blackness to the broken window. He stumbled over a body on the floor just inside the window.

"I think he's dead," Dave said.

Trompet was there an instant later, striking a match.

"Dead as he'll ever be," he said critically. "Plugged right through the head. I never shot a deputy sheriff before, but as long as I got to, it might as well be Sam Dunn. I never did like him."

Sam Dunn lay there on his back. His undershot jaw was sagging; his wide loose mouth was open; blood seeped from a hole in the side of his head.

Trompet struck another match, moved over into the corner. He stooped over to raise something from the floor, and grunted as he set it down with a heavy thump.

"Somebody was smart," he said. "Big leather saddlebags

packed with bars, all ready to move if anybody was strong enough to heft 'em . . . strong like Sam Dunn."

More leather saddlebags lay there on the floor before a dark opening in the rough wooden paneling of the back wall. A desk had been moved away from the spot.

"Bartlett's desk," Dave said as Trompet lighted a third match, opened the leather flap of the saddlebag he had lifted and set down, displaying the dull yellow sheen of the gold bars inside. "Bartlett sat here all day with his feet almost against it. Sam Dunn often was in here to convoy gold shipments down to the express office. Maybe he discovered something on his own hook and counted himself in, or else Bartlett figured he needed Dunn."

"Pretty smart, both of them, anyway," Trompet said admiringly as the match went out.

"They thought they were," Dave said. "Played poor until they could cash in quick and get out. Dunn even owed Colonel Rittenhouse two thousand. I guess he thought that was smart. But it was the loan that took him to see the colonel that night. As deputy sheriff he heard the colonel's suspicions about Bartlett then. He knew Bartlett was a goner, and himself, too, probably, if the colonel wasn't stopped quick. He killed him and laid the blame on me. That was smart, too. Only not smart enough. It was that loan he didn't need to carry him that put me on his trail through Bartlett."

"He's got a rifle out there in the saddle boot," Trompet said. "Probably the same caliber that killed Bartlett."

"Uhn-huh," Dave agreed. "He did that. Things got away from him. He brought me back here to hang. That got me after Bartlett. He finally was forced to arrest Bartlett. He had to stop Bartlett before the fellow weakened in jail."

The watchman, not badly wounded, had crept back in while they talked. "By God, you're right!" he said.

Dave sighed. "It's clear," he said. "But they'll probably hang me before it all comes out. I think I killed Dunn, too, which won't help any."

In the darkness Trompet said: "There'll be a crowd here in a little while. I killed Dunn. Get it? I've got the story straight now, an' I believe it. Climb out the back window there an' hunt cover until morning. I'll have the lynching hunger stopped by then. They'll be welcoming you back with a brass band before I'm through."

"I'll play it out with you two!" the watchman said.

"Thanks!" Trompet struck another match. He said to Dave: "Why didn't you say you were wounded?"

"Didn't want to delay anything that might help me." Dave chuckled as he moved to the window. "I'll lay low like you say. I've got a sudden feeling that this isn't my night to hang."

"Where you goin' to hide?" Trompet asked.

Dave paused, astride the window sill. "At the colonel's house," he said. "I want to return that horse and hat, and tell the colonel's daughter what's happened. Maybe she'll think a little kindly of me and fix my arm. I didn't hear what she said when you left."

Trompet snorted. "Sounds like you must have. She said you looked too nice to hang. Go on back there, Worth. Your troubles is only started."

SMART GUY

The year 1946 saw T.T. Flynn getting paid more money per word by pulp magazines like *Dime Detective* and entering into new markets entirely. He published "Gambler's Lady" in *The American Magazine*, continued contributing fiction to *Argosy* (which had become a slick-paper magazine in 1943), and sold "Smart Guy" to *Short Stories*. Although *Short Stories*, like *Blue Book*, was still a pulp magazine, it was noted for the literary quality of its fiction. Flynn did not title this story before his agent submitted it (the manuscript was accepted on March 13, 1946), and accordingly the title given it by Dorothy McIlwraith, for years the highly capable editor of *Short Stories*, has been retained. The experience Flynn had gained as a young man working for the railroad in Maryland stood him in good stead with this and so many other stories.

I

It had been a long way back to the clean smell of sand and sage and drifting engine smoke over the Desert City yards. George Brandon made it a longer way by detouring from the Army via Central America and points south. He couldn't have said exactly why at the time.

Tonight he squatted comfortably near a stack of cross-ties, pulled leisurely on a cigarette, and looked across the dark yards toward the twinkling lights of Desert City. Tomorrow he'd be over the high Porcupine grades to the east, in Junction City, where he had started. He had wired Rosie O'Grady from Frisco a week before. Six hours ago he had wired Rosie again, collect, that they'd be married now any day. That collect wire would take a little explaining.

A quiet voice off to the right drew nearby attention. The speaker was invisible in the night, but, as George Brandon understood the evenly spoken words, he masked the cigarette tip in a palm.

"You took the money and knew there was no backing out!"

A switch engine, shunting cars nearby, had masked the approaching steps. Now with the engine briefly quiet, a second man mumbled a reply. The words cut off abruptly on a gasping note.

The engine jerked slack out of a string of cars and its stack exhaust punched loudly at the night as George peered toward the strangers. Slowly, silently, he stood up.

Wheel flanges squealed over switches. Smoky light from the engine tank probed across the maze of tracks. A low switch stand took vague shape—and the two men who should have been at that spot were not there.

George reached the switch stand as the engine light moved away. In murky darkness his foot nudged a man's sprawled body. He bent and found an arm, and it had a slack foot, all too familiar these past years.

A brief match flare held low showed a stranger in the middle thirties, wearing a blue suit of fair quality, neatly pressed. The skull over the left ear had been bashed in by a terrific blow.

George Brandon was a chunky, muscular, even-tempered

young man who avoided trouble when he could. This cold-blooded killing was a shock. It should be reported, and that meant delay. Witnesses often were locked up. George stood uncertainly, trying to decide what to do.

The matter was settled by a flashlight stabbing out suddenly behind him. He turned quickly, and a second light reached for him, closing in, also. A voice called: "Don't move!"

The bobbing lights reached him and a hand grabbed his left arm. "What's going on here?"

The second man put light on the body and caught George's other arm, demanding: "You two have a fight?" He shook the arm. "Where's your gun?"

George stood slackly, letting them be rough. He could almost smile at the mistake they were making. "I found him like this," he explained carefully. "Another man was talking to him a few minutes ago. Must have run behind that string of gondolas over there. If you move fast, you might find him."

"Listen to him, Ed!" jeered the man at George's left. "We run over there, and he runs the other way! Swing him around."

"Do you two work for the railroad?" George asked hopefully.

"Shut up!"

Hands frisked expertly under his coat and came out. "Look, Ed!"

Both flashlights centered on a small automatic. It was an old gun, badly abused. George stared speechlessly as the man sniffed the muzzle.

"Been fired, Ed! Say . . . is he the one who knocked that guy off tonight?"

George blurted: "I didn't. . . ."

Ed slapped him hard on the mouth, smashing lips into

103

teeth. "We'll talk. Where'd you get the gun?"

"Never saw it before," George denied huskily.

"Take a good look!"

George reached for the gun—and snatched his hand back. His fingerprints had almost transferred to the battered metal. Bruised lips throbbed painfully; his mouth felt dry as he swallowed hard and forced a calm reply. "I see it. You didn't find that gun on me."

The busy switch engine stopped short, and a shunted car rumbled softly along a spur track. Ed cleared his throat. He sounded thoughtful. "Jack, suppose we take him over to the car and radio in about this stiff. Then we can ride out in the country and talk about it. He must have done that job tonight, and met this guy here an' had a quarrel with him."

"First," Jack insisted, "he takes a good look at this gun." He twisted George's arm. "Take it!"

"I can see it," George refused stubbornly.

Ed, on the other side, was a big man with a raspy voice. "Tough guy, huh?"

His quick move telegraphed his purpose. George ducked. A short-armed hook grazed the side of his jaw. George sucked an unsteady breath. This was a sample of what waited on the ride. They were framing him and meant to make it stick, fingerprints and all. You heard about such things. Nothing else, George decided rather desperately, could make it much worse now. There lay one dead man. These two spoke of a second dead man. They evidently had the murder gun and needed fingerprints.

George Brandon—killer. He had no alibi, witnesses, money. He'd come into Desert City on a freight train and had meant to go out on one, riding the caboose, as soon as the Sunrise Limited cleared the station.

"Take the gun!" Ed ordered.

George sucked in another soft breath. They thought they were tough, and they were clumsy. A good man at the trade of violence could have taken them long ago. The Army had taught well, and George used it in explosive silence. His knee drove into Ed's groin. The big man gasped and doubled over. George already was pivoting back, guessing the other one wouldn't try to slug him with the old automatic.

His upflung arm took the blow, and he had guessed right. They hadn't offered him a loaded weapon. The gun was not fired, and Jack had forgotten to cut off his flashlight.

George whipped a looping smash in past the light. A cheek crunched under his fist. He followed in, hitting again. The target tripped back over a cross-tie end and fell heavily on the steel rail. The flashlight skidded across the ground, its bright beam still on.

George dimly saw the man roll limply off the rail, looking as if he might be the third dead one. Big Ed was still bent over in helpless pain as George bolted. He did not run in panic. Somewhere in the past few years he had learned to think coolly as the going got harder.

Big Ed fired a shot as George reached the first gondola. The bullet *pinged* shrilly off the gondola steel, and he ran in brief safety behind the long string of black cars. At the other end he stopped, panting, and seemed to be alone in the night. Big Ed was evidently not up to running. The yard engine was working some distance away, and a heavier engine was coming on the main line. George weighed quickly what he was going to attempt, and then raced across the yard tracks.

II

The Sunrise Limited was coming, bright-reaching head-light pouring far ahead, stack exhausts blasting as the long drag of heavy coaches slowly picked up speed. George plunged over a shallow ditch and stopped beside the main line, breathing hard. The headlight glared over him. This was the dangerous moment—now as the big engine rushed to him. Steam roared from the engine cylinder and enveloped him in hot, blinding fog. The oily smell of the engine, the deadening cacophony of rods, brasses, cross-heads crashed past.

Half-blinded, George stabbed for the engine hand rail. The metal slapped hard into his palm and almost tore away. He banged helplessly against the engine steps. His foot slipped off the bottom step. Only a frantic clutch at the tank handrail saved him from falling under the tank trucks.

He lurched through the gangway into the dim, warm cab and recognized the engineer. Dave Freeman had been full of dirty little tricks when George had fired for him years back. Still breathing hard, George said: "You opened those cylinder cocks on purpose, Dave! Tried to throw me under the train, didn't you?"

"George Brandon, huh? How'd I know it was you? No deadheads on this engine! Against the rules!"

The fireman slapped George's back and grabbed his hand. It was Pinky Willis, a grinning pint of a man who had been a call boy at the Junction City roundhouse just after George had been call boy.

Dave Freeman scowled at them. "George, you'll have to unload at Holy Joe Creek!"

Pinky protested. "Aw, Dave! You didn't start yelling rule book when I thought another guy hooked on back beyond the yard tower!"

George tightened inside. "Is someone else riding outside tonight?"

"I thought I seen a guy latch on my side," Pinky told him. "Maybe not. But Dave didn't worry about it."

"I'll look on the tank," George decided.

He found a heavy wrench inside the dark bulkhead. Pinky and Dave stared curiously as he climbed the grab irons and sidled back along the top of the rocking tank. The wind caught at him. The back sweep of cinders rattled like fine hail.

Pinky opened the fire door. Red glare leaped back over the coal. George made certain no stranger was riding the top of the tank. He looked down into the blinds, and then, feeling a little sheepish but still wary, he returned to the cab and put the wrench back.

"What's the idea?" Dave Freeman called from the throttle seat.

George shrugged. "You don't like deadheads, Dave. I had a look."

"Having you in my cab is what I don't like," Dave retorted irritably. "I ain't having Andy MacKinnon on my neck for breaking rules."

"What's Andy got to do with it?"

"He's road foreman of engineers now."

Pinky chortled. "What Dave means is . . . he and Andy are courting the same girl."

George smiled at that. "Two roosters eyeing each other,

huh? Who's the girl?"

"Old Pat O'Grady's youngest daughter," Pinky said. "Remember her? The pretty one . . . Rosie."

Dave snapped: "Work your fire instead of your mouth, Pinky, an' we may have steam enough to get up the hill. Next thing you'll be seeing more blue lights."

Dave opened the injector. Steam and boiler feed water growled loudly. Pinky opened the two halves of the fire door and disgustedly indicated dull spots on the sheeting flames where dirty coal was sulking. George stood in numb silence, feeling as if he'd been punched under the belt.

The train was rolling now. The heavy steel tank apron was banging loudly on the cab deck. A main-rod brass slammed in dull rhythm. Wheels, rods, cross-heads made a noisy background to the fast stack exhausts batting hard on the night. They were already in the first light curves and grades of the Porcupine foothills. Dave was holding his valves too wide, wasting steam that Pinky had to make with bad coal. Everything was happening to George Brandon tonight.

George tried to calm his thoughts by changing the subject. "Pinky, what did Dave mean about blue lights?"

"Nothin'." Pinky looked uncomfortable, and then he shrugged. "You'll hear about it, I guess." He motioned George to the fireman's seat and stood beside him. "Remember Three Mile Cut, beyond Porcupine Pass?"

George nodded.

"Last trip east we were out of the cut, rolling slow on the downgrade, when I seen a blue light out to the left," Pinky said.

"I've seen a lot of things up in the Porcupines . . . but no blue lights," George said, smiling at the idea.

"The track runs along the edge of Three Mile Cañon and swings away in that sharp curve," Pinky reminded. "The blue light was just at the curve, back off the right of way, like a blue eye tryin' to tell me something. I called Dave across to look."

"What did Dave say?"

"Nothing until we were at the roundhouse. Then," said Pinky bitterly, "he swore he hadn't seen any blue light. He tried to make me out a screwball."

"How were you feeling at the time, Pinky?"

"There you go!" Pinky said in exasperation. "I don't want to talk about it anyway!"

Pinky had always seemed level-headed. Not a drinking man, either. But a blue light up by Three-Mile Cañon, in the middle of the night, was hard to take. His own troubles prodded George. He had to ask one question.

"Which one has the high ball with Rosie?"

"My guess is she ain't hung out a green signal yet," Pinky said, grinning again. "But that's why you got to unload at Holy Joe Creek, George, when we take the hole to let the Westliner down the hill. Dave ain't giving Andy McKinnon a chance to derail him with a broken rule." Pinky chuckled. "Them two bristle when they think about each other."

George tried to smile. He had an idea the grimace looked sickly. Morosely he watched Pinky check lubricator and firebox.

Dave had pulled goggles over his eyes and was leaning out the cab window. The heavy mountain engine was wheeling into the grades. Curves were sharper. Huge rocky slopes thrust up to right and left. The long drag of jewel-lighted coaches and Pullmans trailed sinuously around the curves.

This, George thought miserably, was everything he'd been coming back to. This—and Rosie O'Grady. The truth of it now was flat in his mouth. He'd detoured too far and too long.

Pinky joined him again and offered a cigarette and cupped

a match. George reluctantly asked: "Trouble of some kind in Desert City tonight, wasn't there?"

"I heard talk at the roundhouse," Pinky agreed. "Some guy held up a big poker game in a back room of a pool hall. One of the players got shot through an eye. Good shooting, I'd say. The killer got away, too. They say he had on a handkerchief mask. Medium build fellow . . . about your build." Pinky chuckled and slapped George's arm. "Maybe it was you, George!"

Pinky was still amused by the thought as he looked at the steam gauge and firebox. George sat on Pinky's jouncing seat and brooded. By now the law might be waiting in Junction City for the man who'd caught the engine of the Limited. George Brandon—killer.

He was still brooding when Dave made air reductions for Holy Joe siding. With a wave to Pinky, George swung off on the left side, and stood watching closely as the heavy coaches rolled slowly past. There was no sign of a man riding outside the train. Pinky must have been mistaken.

George stood there, half decided to let the train go on without him. But Holy Joe Creek was a wild spot. The mountains around were worse. Eastbound trains mostly took the hole here. West-running schedules came fast down the grades with the line cleared ahead. A man afoot at Holy Joe might have to walk out or swing on another run east.

But—if he rode the Limited to Junction City, he might duck pursuit and catch a run back west, even to the coast. He might get back south of Panama where a stranger could make a new start. George walked toward the flagman's lantern, and he had tight-wound feelings that disaster was poised and waiting.

III

He spoke to the surprised flagman with false heartiness. "I dropped off the engine." He walked slowly up the right side of the train to the conductor's light, fingering three pennies in his pocket. All he had. The pennies suddenly reminded him of three dead men. George jerked the hand out of the pocket and wondered uneasily if panic wasn't creeping in.

The conductor was Dad Benton, a thin, spry old man who peered past his lifted lantern. "By golly, George Brandon!"

"I got off the engine, Dad. Haven't a pass yet. Any spare cushions inside?"

"No money?" Dad asked shrewdly.

"Well . . . no."

Dad thought a moment. A thin smile deepened his wrinkles. "You can ride section seven, in the car ahead. The Pullman conductor is Bill Cleary. He'll look the other way. But you'll have to sit up, George."

"I'm not sleepy, Dad. Thanks a lot."

George wondered heavily as he entered the Pullman if he'd ever feel sleepy again. Dad's smile had been rather queer, too. But Dad wouldn't double-cross an old friend. He was probably safe on the Limited until it slowed for the Junction City yards. After that he'd have to move fast.

Section seven was empty, save for a light zipper bag on the forward seat. George sat down, sensing something peculiar about the two men across the aisle. They sat stiffly side by side, not at all friendly looking. The nearest man turned a cold scrutiny as George sat down. In a moment his companion leaned forward, looking also.

That second man by the window had a leaden-faced, malevolent stare from under a down-pulled gray hat. The look carried dislike for George Brandon and everyone else in sight.

The other man shifted his left hand. Steel glinted at the wrist. George realized uneasily that they were law officer and prisoner. It was the prisoner who hated anyone free of handcuffs.

The officer appeared hard-boiled and efficient. He seemed suspicious of the man who'd come in without baggage, between the stations, to sit opposite them.

The law only a foot or two away! George drew a slow breath. The tightness was building in him again. Was this the reason Dad Benton had smiled queerly?

The porter was making up berths at the front of the car. Passengers moved back and forth between the washrooms. The Westliner came down the hill with deep-toned air horns blasting far ahead, the latest thing in Diesel-electric speed and luxury. It rushed past with a roar of big motors and a brightly lighted flash of the streamlined future.

George drew a slow breath. If he were only on the Westliner now, speeding west to the Coast, money in his pocket, a safe, calm future ahead. . . .

Dave Freeman whistled in the flagman and took slack out of the train with skill George had to admire. The Limited crept out on the main line and picked up speed behind a heavy throttle. A young lady came along the aisle and gasped audibly, and, as George looked up, she kissed him.

"You big goop, where have you been?" Rosie O'Grady demanded breathlessly.

George gulped and kissed her back. It was like fire and ice.

He caught Rosie's hand and grinned foolishly as they sat side by side, and then George dropped his hand.

"Don't you belong up in the cab with Dave Brennan?"

"Oh!" Rosie said. She was prettier than ever, with the same tip-tilt nose and deep-blue eyes that could go stormy. "Say the rest of it!" Rosie challenged.

"Two-timing me," George accused bitterly. "Dave and Andy MacKinnon. All the time I thought. . . ."

"You thought!" Rosie said coldly. "What was *I* thinking while you pranced around strange countries?"

"I was only seeing a few things."

"No doubt. Did you take all their names and addresses?"

"Now, look, Rosie. . . ."

"And you had the nerve to wire me, collect, you were finally condescending to come home and marry me! Collect!"

"I got in a dice game in Frisco."

"Did I ask for an explanation?"

"Anyway, I can't marry you now, Rosie."

"You certainly can't!" Rosie agreed coldly.

"I can explain, but I'd better not," George said miserably.

"You'd better not waste breath trying. I'm not interested, George Brandon. Good bye."

"Rosie. . . ."

George watched dejectedly as the angry back of Rosie's head swept toward the dressing room. He scowled at the two men across the aisle, who'd been watching.

The law officer stared back without expression. He seemed to be thinking deeply. George guessed the man was riffling through a mental rogue's gallery, trying to place him. At least, he would remember George Brandon's face now.

Rosie stayed out of sight. Dad Benton came through, and stopped. He looked shyly pleased. "Where's Rosie O'Grady?"

113

"Powdering her nose, I guess."

Dad Benton chuckled. "She's a fine girl, George. I was at her father's wedding. I'm looking for an invitation to Rosie's wedding."

George nodded glumly. He didn't feel like talking about Rosie's wedding. He wondered whether it would be to Andy MacKinnon or Dave Freeman, and then tried to forget about it by listening to the engine. They were on the high grades now, roaring through tunnels and lurching around sharp curves with wheel flanges screaming. It took the heaviest mountain engines to haul these grades without double-heading. George automatically ticked off the bad spots.

There was Jackknife Hill, with the tunnel at the top. . . . Dave barely got over. And then Parson's Loop, where snow sheds and fences could barely keep the line open in winter. Dave slipped his driving wheels badly on the steep grade of Parson's Loop. Finally there was the heavy haul up Porcupine grade to the tunnel—and then they were over the hump.

The tearing stack exhausts quieted. Brake shoes ground on the wheels. The heavy train worked cautiously into the first downgrade.

The coach was dim, passengers in berths, the porter out of sight. George stood restlessly, and the law officer gave him a sharp look. He ignored the two men and walked to the vestibule ahead.

Noise clattered, slammed, and roared in the bright-lighted, dusty space between the cars. But here he was alone. George leaned against the left-hand door and stared moodily through the dusty glass into the passing night.

He had more strongly than ever a feeling of being trapped by forces beyond his command. He'd read somewhere that a man's life was determined outside himself and had never believed it. You made your own life. Now he was confused, rebellious, and helpless against facts.

When Rosie left the train at Junction City, he'd be the one in the yards, hoping for a quick, furtive ride back west. Leaving all he'd hoped and planned for. George Brandon—killer. The train echoed in a long cut. In the door glass he saw Rosie come out into the vestibule and stop at sight of him. He turned to her reluctantly, and had to speak loudly through the train racket.

"You can have your seat. I'll stay out here."

Rosie moved closer. Her blue eyes had the stony look again. "Who said I care where you sit, George Brandon?" Rosie swallowed. "Or what you do?"

George shrugged.

Rosie swallowed again. "Did I ask what you've been doing all the time you wouldn't come home?"

"Now, Rosie . . . you know. . . ."

"Don't make excuses, George! Did I even mention *señoritas* and grass skirts and . . . ?"

"They don't wear grass skirts," George said.

"So you found out all about it!"

A lurch of the train threw Rosie against him. George went a little giddy as he steadied her slim figure. He almost kissed her, and remembered what lay ahead for George Brandon, and turned back to the dusty door glass.

Rosie's voice sounded choked. "You weren't even interested enough to ask what I was doing on this train."

"With Dave Freeman on the engine?" George said, not looking at her.

The train rolled out of the long cut. He realized it had been Three Mile Cut. The train was now skirting the deep black trench that was Three Mile Cañon. He'd looked countless times into that deep cañon, and in memory now could see white water boiling over the jagged rocks below.

T. T. Flynn

Rosie was speaking indignantly at his elbow. "If you think, George Brandon. . . ."

He missed the rest of it as a small blue light appeared out there in the night, whisking back out of sight as the train rolled on.

George yanked the door open, forgetting the abrupt curve here. A twist of the vestibule almost threw him out into space. Rosie caught his coat. "George, don't jump!"

She clung desperately as George leaned out into the whip of wind, trying to see the blue light again, but only coaches bulging out around the rim of the curve were visible.

"Please, George!" Rosie wailed.

Engine smoke whipped past. George swore under his breath. A blue light here by the cañon! A light like Pinky Willis had seen! Then he caught his breath and leaned out farther.

The door at the rear of this same Pullman had opened. A dark bundle that looked like a body had tumbled out into space. George was sure it was a body.

A man appeared on the steps, as he looked, and swung off and landed with grotesque, leaping steps, and fell and disappeared. A second man appeared on the steps and swung off.

"Look out, Rosie!" George said hoarsely, shouldering back and slamming the door.

Rosie stammered. "Wh-what's wrong?"

George left her there and ran back into the Pullman. The long-curtained aisle was dim and quiet—and the two men who'd been sitting across the aisle from him were gone!

The quick helpless feeling that followed left George's mouth dry. He knew where the men were and what it meant to George Brandon. The other passengers had been asleep when he walked to the vestibule. Not even Rosie had seen him. Once more he had no witnesses and no alibi, and he was

116

left to explain what had happened to the men.

This was almost as bad as the Desert City trouble. It would all be hooked up together. He had the trapped feeling again as he ran to the rear vestibule.

The door was still open. The train was picking up speed as he went to the bottom step and poised there, without thinking much about what he was doing. It seemed to be planned for him. He heard the vestibule door open. It was Rosie, and she looked frightened when she saw him on the step.

"Tell Dad Benton that cop and prisoner are gone!" George called.

"Please, George! Come back here!"

Light from the train rushed across fairly even ground beside the track, and George swung out and down.

IV

He landed hard, hurled into great strides by the momentum. His right foot struck an uneven spot. He tripped, fell hard, and slid and rolled to a stop.

He lay there getting breath back as the train rolled past. The thick night closed in, and he got stiffly to his feet. The low roar of the Limited was fading around the next curve, and the solid quiet of the mountains dropped down. From far slopes the thin clamor of coyotes drifted across the stars as he stood motionless, breathing softly.

This spot was at least a mile from where the men had unloaded. George wondered if that first limp object pushed into space had been the law officer. It must have been.

The prisoner, of course, was one of the two men who had followed. George recalled the gray-faced stare. He moistened dry lips. No need to wonder what that man would do with a gun.

He could guess what must have happened. Somewhere on the train another man had been riding, waiting for the exact moment to help the prisoner escape. Pinky's blue light must have been the signal.

Rather dismally George wondered how big a fool he was. He was unarmed. There was no help in this part of the mountains. He wondered what would have happened if he'd been sitting across the aisle, or if Rosie had been there, and thought he knew.

The knowledge stirred a slow cold anger that, queerly, made him feel better as he started back up the track. He was in more trouble, and he knew who had made this trouble, and he could find them.

They'd be watching. Guns might blast without warning, from any point of the night. But the past years had taught this sort of thing well. George walked at the edge of the rock ballast, on dirt, making little noise. Now and then he stopped and listened intently.

He tried to think with their minds. A careful plan was being carried out. The blue light was proof of that. At least one more man had been handling the light. So there were three men, and perhaps more ahead. They'd be moving fast. By tomorrow roads out of the Porcupines would be watched.

They wouldn't, George guessed, try to hole up in the mountains. That sort of thing worked well if there was no sound. In a case like this the mountains would quickly turn into a trap.

Pleased with that reasoning, George stopped again. The coyotes had quieted. Up the high slopes wind murmured

118

softly in pine tops—and there was a closer, metallic whisper, on the right that seemed new. Only a railroad man could have placed the sound instantly. George dropped down and put an ear to the cold steel rail, and got it clearly. Wheels coming down the grade.

It took a railroad man to add that up fast. There was a tool shed and a hand car or a motor car just this side of Three Mile Cut. At least it had been there since George could remember, and probably still was. He was off the right of way, searching wildly, while that ran through his mind. He found the kind of rock he wanted, large and flat. Skin abraded from his fingers as he clawed the rock out of the ground. He grunted with effort as he staggered back in the track and placed the rock, and retreated back downgrade.

Now he could hear the wheels whispering swiftly. And still no light. But a chill held him. Suppose it was a track inspector following up the Limited? George backed off beside the track and stopped trembling. If he wrecked an honest man. . . . You had to be a railroad man, too, to understand how that would be.

The wheel sounds grew louder, louder—and, when the crash came, George jumped in spite of himself. The low-speeding car did exactly what he'd planned, derailing and striking red sparks as it plunged off the right of way. Wild cries of fright cut off quickly. George thought the car turned over a time or two before it stopped. Then a man began to cry oaths of pain. Other voices joined in, and George sucked a quick breath of relief. A flashlight came on, stabbing wildly around, and George retreated downgrade. He was still unarmed.

A second light came on. The men who held them could move around. The lights probed at the track and at the wrecked car. George saw the rock discovered and lifted away.

The light beams swept frantically around, searching the night.

He dropped flat, watching. He counted at least three men moving around now. One, when light struck him, seemed to be limping badly. Then George lifted his head with a startled movement, listening.

His name had been called. Impossible! But it came again, downgrade in the distance, striking faintly but clearly through the thin mountain air. A girl's voice calling: "George! Oh, George!"

The flashlights cut off. George swore softly, got to his feet, and ran toward the voice with the first deep, panicky fear he'd known tonight. He didn't doubt it was Rosie, because he knew Rosie. She would be alone, because she showed no light, and he had only his hands between her and those desperate men who'd also heard her calling.

It was in a way like a nightmare. Rosie called again, and heard his steps, and her voice went unsteadily out far ahead. "Is that you, George?"

"Shut up, Rosie." George reached her with a rush and caught her arm roughly. He was panting, heart hammering. "You little fool. Get up the mountainside with me quick. They heard you. Keep your mouth shut."

He'd never talked to Rosie like this, nor had anyone else. The savage urge of his arm lifted her over the rails, into a stumbling run off the right of way and up the first steep slope through scattered undergrowth.

The slope grew steeper. Rosie slipped. George dug his heels in and rushed her on, and they reached the first pines and deep carpet of dead needles.

"You're hurting my arm," Rosie gasped.

"Keep quiet," George whispered furiously. But he stopped and released her arm and looked back down the steep slope as he tried to catch breath.

A bobbing flashlight was probing down the tracks, over the spot where Rosie would have been. The light went on a little. A sharp voice called: "Who's there?" Then the voice shouted impatiently up the track. "If this thing's wrecked, hurry up! It's a long walk."

The light shifted up the mountainside, reaching among the trees. "Sit down," George ordered under his breath. He crouched, waiting, and the voices drifted up to them clearly. One man was cursing, limping badly.

"That rock never rolled there! It was put there! There's someone around here!"

"So what. We ain't got time to start running around in these damned mountains!"

"That was a woman's voice, I tell you."

"No dames for you tonight, Rocky. If she's smart, she'll keep outta the way."

Rosie started to speak, huskily: "That's. . . ."

"Shut up," George whispered fiercely, and Rosie fell quiet.

There were three men and two flashlights, and probably three guns. One of them said: "How far is it?" He was answered: "About ten miles from here. Maybe fifteen. And if we ain't on the way by daylight, it'll be too bad!" Then the voices began to fade.

"All right, Rosie. What are you doing here?" George demanded under his breath. "Speak low," he warned.

"I told the porter what you said, and pulled the air and jumped off," Rosie said meekly. She had never sounded so subdued. "George . . . that Rocky, his name is Rocky Scholl. He'a an escaped killer. A . . . hoodlum. Dad Benton told me. The man was taking him back to Chicago to serve a life sentence."

"So you jump off and try to find him. Didn't I have enough trouble? Listen . . . they'd have shot you quick and talked about it later."

"I was afraid you'd get killed," Rosie said miserably.

"Butting in. Having your own way."

"Well, I like. . . ."

"Who asked what you liked?" George cut off her indignation. He was still shaky when he thought of what might have happened to Rosie. "If I'm right, and I think I'm right," George muttered, "one of those hoodlums grabbed the train after it left the Desert City station . . . and I've got to get my hands on him."

Rosie caught her breath. "Dad Benton was laughing about a man who almost missed the train. He caught the observation platform and climbed over. He had his ticket bought, and said he'd gone for a walk and forgot the time. He was in the car back of me. Why do you have to get him, George?"

"He killed a man in the Desert City yards. They're trying to blame it on me."

"Who is?" Rosie faltered.

"The Desert City police. I broke away and caught the engine as it came by. And thanks to you and Dave Freeman and Andy MacKinnon, I had to get off the engine at Holy Joe Creek, so Andy couldn't catch Dave breaking a rule. And I get caught right in the middle on this escape. They'll never believe now that I didn't help. That law officer is dead, I think. And someone held up a poker game in Desert City tonight and killed a man, and I'm getting blamed for that."

"I wish you'd stop talking about Dave and Andy, George." Rosie caught her breath again. "I . . . I was hoping someone would write you about it, and you'd hurry home."

"For Pete's sake, I can't worry about those two now. Even," George added darkly, "if you did have to follow Dave

Freeman around at his work."

"There you go again," said Rosie, sounding almost tearful. "You've changed . . . running all over the world."

George started to tell her how it had happened, about the deep restlessness that had urged: *Look once at it while you can, before you go back and marry Rosie and live happily ever after on the Mountain Division. Last chance to see it, Georgie, now.*

Something kept him quiet.

"Those *señoritas*," Rosie said. "I know."

"Um-um," George said. He thought of some of the girls he had seen, and he smiled wryly. Rosie was like a spirited young queen in contrast. "Not so hot," he said carelessly. He coughed. "That is, not all of them."

"I'd rather not hear about it, George," Rosie said with dignity.

"All right. But keep quiet, Rosie. I've got to think. I'm in plenty trouble."

"If you killed anyone, you had a reason for it," Rosie said huskily. "I knew you were in trouble, George, when you sent that collect wire. The plane that stopped at Desert City left in twenty minutes, and I caught it. And then I couldn't find you."

"I went broke in a crap game in Frisco," George said absently. "I was trying to. . . ." He broke off. This wasn't the time to tell Rosie he'd been trying to win a lot of money for an extra-special, luxurious honeymoon. "I'm in plenty of trouble. It's bad. Didn't seem much hope until those guys unloaded from the train." He stood up, breathing deeply. "Now, I don't know. There's a chance. . . ."

"Can I stand up?" Rosie asked meekly.

"I guess so. They seem to be gone. Ten miles . . . maybe fifteen. . . . I wonder where they're going." George stood, thinking hard.

"I never thought you'd kill anyone," Rosie said haltingly. "You have changed, George."

"Cow Creek?" George exclaimed.

"What?"

"Those old Cow Creek places and abandoned cabins," George said, getting excited. "There isn't another place within fifteen miles of here."

"Oh, that place," Rosie said. "That's where Tommy Goodman and his friends used to fly to last fall, when they hunted deer."

George caught her arm. "Rosie. Did you say *fly?*"

V

"George! You startled me! Yes. They leveled off a landing strip on the Cow Creek flats, and some of the men from Junction City fly in there to fish and hunt in season. There isn't any way to get an automobile in, and the trail is almost impassable from the railroad. But they can fly in easily."

"And fly out easily," George said, trying to keep excitement out of his voice. "Who all knows about it?"

"Why, everybody, I guess. It was written up in a hunting magazine last spring, with pictures and everything. I read it. Tommy Goodman's picture. . . ."

"Yes, yes," George said impatiently. "Now, look, Rosie, this is terribly serious. Will you do exactly what I tell you?"

"Yes," Rosie said steadily, "and I don't believe you're a killer."

"I am right now," George said grimly. "The facts say so.

Now, listen, Rosie. I think those men unloaded from the train up here because it always runs slow around that cañon curve. And they had a trackman's car there to coast down to the Cow Creek trail. If they'd jump off and let the car roll on, it'd take some time to guess where they'd gone. Get it?"

"I . . . I think so," Rosie said. "But they were walking."

"I wrecked 'em," George said with some satisfaction. "They won't be back that way. But don't take chances. Sit in the bushes down there and keep quiet."

"Yes, George."

"Dad Benton might stop the train and telephone to Junction City. At least when he gets in, he'll give the alarm. They'll get help up here if it takes a special engine. But news might not get here until well after daybreak. That's when you show yourself. Not before. Tell them to look for a dead or injured law officer this side of the tool shack. Warn them that Rocky Scholl and two pals have headed for Cow Creek, evidently to fly out and vanish. Tell 'em to get to Cow Creek fast. Understand?"

"Yes," Rosie said obediently. "Where will you be, George? Or shall I tell them?"

"I wish you wouldn't forget it," George said. He cleared his throat. "I'll be waiting at Cow Creek, too, if . . . well, if nothing happens. I'm going to cut over the shoulder of the mountain here. You'll do that exactly? No more and no less?"

"Yes, George."

"Kiss me."

Rosie came against him, clinging hard. She'd never kissed him like this. It shook George. He discovered that Rosie's cheeks were wet, and it almost unnerved him. She'd been chattering along—and crying in the dark.

" 'Bye," George said gruffly. He left her there and went up through the pines with long strides.

125

★ ★ ★ ★ ★

George had hunted deer up here a few times, but trying to cross the shoulder of the mountain fast in darkness was another thing. He was quickly panting, and then streaming sweat as the steep slopes went up and up, until he was afraid he was going wrong and making for the high peaks. He bore left harder, stumbling now and then on uncertain footing, rough branches whipping his face.

Then suddenly he was at the edge of the Big Burn, where black tree stubs thrust gaunt char toward the stars, and he knew where he was. The late moon edged up in the far east and helped. George cut across the slopes, downward now, away from the tangle of fallen trunks and lush small-growth in the Burn. He struck a seepage swath and slipped and struggled through muck that once was halfway to a knee. He slipped and fell in the mess, and got up swearing, and went on faster.

This was taking longer than he thought. If there was a plane at Cow Creek and it got off with its passengers, George Brandon might as well keep going. Not that it would help much now. George began to run.

He was sucking great, shuddering breaths when the slope pitched down steeper and he heard the low drone of falling water. He stopped, and weakness came at the calves of his legs and up past his knees toward hammering heart.

"Fool!" George said hoarsely, trying to get breath. "Knock yourself out before you get there!"

That water was Cow Creek Falls. The climbing moon washed pale silver into the valley shadows far below, where the water wandered through Cow Creek flats. Dawn, George guessed, was not far away. He went down the mountains with long, loose strides, dreading to hear the distant racket of a plane engine warming up. Once airborne, they'd have the world around to vanish in, any state, Mexico, Canada. He'd made himself believe there must be a plane waiting on Cow Creek flats. There was no other place to go from the railroad, no other line of escape from that planned break-out near Three-Mile Cañon.

He reached the logged-off slopes near the flats—and stopped short, nerves tightening, pulses picking up. Far off to the left a firefly had winked. It glinted again as he watched—an electric firefly in a man's hand, probing the trail in to the flats. He wanted to run again, and made himself go carefully, with as little noise as possible. Down the last slopes and past the rotting, caved-in cabins of the old mining days. Cow Creek water glinted against the moonlight—and George dropped flat with sudden reflex action as twin suns blazed in his direction from the lower end of the flats, and then cut off.

Sighing softly with relief, George stood up. A waiting plane's wing lights had signaled. He could see the flashlight beam at the other end of the flats waving back. There were four men now, including the pilot, and time was running out. Four armed men! They'd all be wary of suspicious sounds or movements. George was running lightly out across the flats as he accepted that.

A man was hard to see in the distance, even in the faint moonlight. George hoped desperately he was not visible just yet. He found the crude-scraped runway and turned toward the plane, trotting on his toes. If the wing lights came on again, he'd be in the full glare, a perfect target.

He could see the low-wing cabin plane now. A blob of movement stirred at the right wing tip and stepped toward him.

"Get it started!" George called.

A flash beam bored out toward him. George waved,

calling again. "Hurry!"

"Who is it?"

"Rocky's hurt! We're followed!"

The pilot cut off the light and lingered, calling as George approached: "You say Scholl's hurt?"

"Yes," George panted angrily.

He was angry, curiously, because the man had put the light on him. The men at the far end of the flats could see him, too. He thought he heard a shout from one of them.

"What are they saying?" the pilot asked as George reached him.

"We'll see," George said huskily. "Lemme have that light to signal 'em."

He ran the light over the pilot as he turned and saw the gun belt and gun, with a holster flap fastened down. The pilot turned, also, so that the gun was on the other side. He was a muscular man, taller than George, tan jacket open, plaid shirt open at the neck, and dark beard rubble on a heavy jaw.

A hard customer, George guessed—and try and get that gun out of the holster without starting a furious fight that might last until the other men reached them, or the pilot got the gun out and used it.

"What are they yelling?" the pilot asked impatiently. "Ain't that mud all over you?"

"Yep," George said. "Here's the light."

"You didn't signal. . . ."

George hit him as only a desperate man could hit. He struck with the war years and the future, and the stark certainty that George Brandon was a dead man tonight or a killer before the law if he bobbled this. He had the range and the weight to do it. The sodden crunch of his fist upon the man's stubbled jaw had a whiplash sound. But that was probably nerves. The way the man spun and collapsed wasn't nerves.

"I signaled!" George said. "How do you like it, brother?" He went after the gun and got it, and felt better as the cool steel automatic nestled in his hand.

One flashlight was on the runway now, bobbing rapidly toward the plane. George caught the pilot's arm and dragged him off the runway. He was still panting, but he felt cool now—cool as a killer in action.

He searched quickly on the scraped-off rubble and found a large rock and ran to the plane. The wing had a metal skin that rang loudly and dented, and stubbornly defied the water-rounded rock. George swore and located the wing tank cap and fired down through the wing. The rich smell of high-octane gas rushed up.

His matches were soggy, useless. George hurled the box to the ground and ran back to the pilot. He clawed a windproof lighter from the tan jacket pocket.

The first running man shouted: "Davis! Is that you?"

George stepped toward the plane and snapped the lighter and tossed it. He saw the wan glow bounce under the wind and start to vanish. Then exploding flame balled out in a blinding gush. He ducked. The hot blow scorched past, and George ran toward the pilot.

Flames were whooshing skyward. The red glare was out over the flats as George dragged the pilot farther away.

He heard the thin lash of a bullet close, and the gun report. The man who'd been running was standing in the reaching light, shooting at him. George grinned. He suddenly felt peacefully content, that wracking trip across the high slopes justified. He had them now on Cow Creek flats.

He dropped comfortably behind the pilot. Cow Creek murmured busily on his left. The man who'd shot at him crouched uncertainly on the runway. The angry flame glow reached out to the other two men, who had halted uncertainly. One had an arm about the other's shoulder. He had been limping badly.

The plane tanks blew up with a dull report. Fire soared toward the stars and scattered widely, and the livid glow rushed far up the mountains. George aimed thoughtfully with the automatic and squeezed the trigger. He'd been a good shot in the Army. He was a good shot now. The man tumbled flat from his wary crouch. He came up into stumbling flight, and a leg caved under him, and he went down again.

The other two men started to retreat. They went slowly, the one hobbling badly, helped each step. That one wouldn't make the railroad, George guessed. The sheriff's men coming in after dawn would meet him or quickly find him.

George drew a slow breath. He didn't feel like a killer, but he must be one at heart, as Rosie would probably always suspect. This wasn't war, but he'd dropped that fellow on the runway without an extra pulse jump.

The high flames began to die down a little. The pilot stirred, and sound grated in his throat. George rolled him face down. The man moved convulsively.

"Keep quiet or I'll blast you," George said coldly.

From an eye corner the pilot saw the gun. He hugged the ground. "OK," he muttered thickly.

"It better be," George said. He liked the sound, cold and threatening. Then he grinned wryly, knowing it wasn't George Brandon speaking, even if he had to shoot.

The flames died down still more. The wounded man lay on the runway, not trying to escape.

"Get up," George ordered the pilot. He looked around and saw the cool gray touch of dawn against the stars. A twinge of anxiety for Rosie, faithfully waiting beside the railroad, touched him. "Grab your hands behind you and walk to that guy on the runway," George said coldly. "The other two are gone, so don't get ideas."

"Say . . . who are you?"

"Shut up!"

The man shut up. George grinned wryly. When they were on the runway, he called to the man ahead: "Throw your gun toward us!"

There was enough light to see the weapon land. George walked the pilot around it, and scooped up a second automatic. The wounded man was scowling uncertainly when they reached him. He recognized the pilot.

"Rocky beat it with Jess," he groaned. "My knee's broke, I think. It's killin' me." He peered at George. "How many are around here?"

"You'd be surprised," George said. The man seemed about his size and build. "You're the one who tried to kill that fellow in the Desert City yards before you hopped the train," George guessed.

The man's startled tension settled that for the time being. Dad Benton could identify him.

"And held up the poker game and shot that player," George added.

The pilot's anger exploded. "Heisted a poker game in Desert City?" He moved threateningly to the seated man. "Cal, did you louse up everything with a stick-up while I waited here?"

George watched, fascinated. It wasn't what the pilot said. It was the way he said it, with merciless judgment, that even under George's gun threat carried chill promise for the future.

The scared man shrunk back a little. "You got it wrong, Slim," he protested urgently. "Williams did it. When we were sure Rocky was on the train, I wired Williams, and then grabbed a plane to Desert City to make sure he got the wire and was ready."

"And he was sticking up poker games?"

"I found him boozed up and hiding in his room, Slim. He'd got tired of waiting and started drinking, and decided to take some easy money out of town. He killed a guy, and then got afraid. The rat never was any good, I guess. He had the ticket to Junction City. I took him for a walk out toward the freight yards, and clipped him on the head, and then just had time to grab the train as it went through the yards. Williams must have run to the cops and squealed. I should have killed him. Damn it . . . I tried to."

"You never can tell," George said. "Tell the sheriff about it when he gets here. He might believe you." George cleared his throat. "It's either you or Williams about that poker game and dead man."

"The money's still in his room. The rat won't hang that on me." The man groaned. "My knee's bleeding."

George cocked his head, listening. "Planes' motors," he said.

The pilot looked to the high slopes, where dawn was creeping past the stars. "Yeah," he said. "I figured they'd get here about dawn if the boys got Rocky off the train, and someone at Junction City thought fast enough about Cow Creek. It'd be smart to look here first, anyway."

George cleared his throat. "Yeah, I guess it was smart," he agreed. The thought left him feeling warm and confident inside. George Brandon—smart guy.

The planes droned over the high slopes and dipped toward the flats. The first one buzzed the runway and smoldering wreck, banked sharply, and came in low over their heads, landing hard and rolling toward the other end of the runway as the other two planes circled.

Men jumped out with rifles and ran back toward them.

"OK!" George yelled when they were in earshot. "I've got two of them!"

Four men. The first man, tall, lanky, bare headed, gray in the growing dawn, wore the sheriff's star and carried a repeating rifle and wore a holstered revolver.

"Are you George Brandon?" he panted.

"Yes," George said. "There's two men heading back toward the railroad you'd better catch. There's a girl back there, waiting, and I wouldn't like to think. . . ."

"If you mean Miss O'Grady," the sheriff said, still breathing fast, "she's probably in Junction City by now. She ran out shortly after you left her and stopped a track inspector's motor car. He telephoned Junction City and took her on. We got these planes started as quick as we could."

"I told her to wait," George said. "Might have seen more trouble. That's just like Rosie."

"Who's Rosie?" the wounded man asked fretfully.

"She's my girl," George said. The words startled him, and he realized they were true. "We're going to be married," George added with growing confidence. A warm glow ran through him and he repeated it. "Going to be married right away," he said.

Deep down in his thoughts George added to himself, confidently: *And live happily always on the Mountain Division. No more running off to see the world. No more detours.*

THE PIE RIVER

When Fred Glidden began writing Western fiction in the mid 1930s (he would use the pseudonym Luke Short), he and Ted Flynn had the same landlord, who introduced the two writers to each other. Flynn's agent was Marguerite E. Harper, and she became Fred Glidden's agent, as she became the agent of Fred's brother, Jon Glidden, when he began writing Western stories under the pseudonym Peter Dawson. In late 1936 Harper concluded a package deal with A. A. Wyn of Magazine Publishers to buy a pre-agreed number of words (i.e., stories) from her stable of writers. Wyn published both *Western Trails* and *Western Aces*. Beginning in the November, 1936 issue of *Western Trails*, stories by these three authors began appearing. According to Ted Flynn's ledger book, Harper sold his story, "The Pie River," to *Western Aces* in July, 1937 as part of this package deal. Flynn was paid $225.00. In the event, the story appeared instead in *Western Trails* (12/37) under the title "The Pistol Prodigal." For its appearance here, the author's original title has been restored.

I
"A HOT-HEADED POSSE"

"Put a bullet in my belly," Steve Cochrane taunted. "See what good it will do you." Between his uplifted arms, Steve Cochrane eyed the men who had crowded into the half-ruined adobe hut.

"It'd give me pleasure," Reeves, the sheriff, gritted.

A long-waisted cowman growled: "It'd probably save somebody a heap of trouble."

Up in the right-hand corner of the room, where the adobe bricks had fallen in, the late afternoon sun drove a golden lance of color through tangled cobwebs. Buzzing flies made pelting darts of movement up there in the stagnant heat under the sagging ceiling boards.

A pack rat had left trash in one corner; the windows had long been broken; the door hung crazily by one bent hinge. The dusty surface of the dirt floor gritted under restless, high-heeled boots. Steve knew that the thread of his life was no stronger than the strands of cobweb up there under the ceiling.

Caleb Reeves, the sheriff, was in a cold fury, and Reeves had never been noted for his mildness. For sixteen years, or maybe it was twenty-six years, the Pie River country had known the name of Caleb Reeves. Steve Cochrane had known it as a boy. Steve had stood on the outskirts of Costerville, the county seat, and watched Caleb Reeves lead posses out after lawbreakers.

In those days Reeves's short, black, upstanding hair had

135

been stiff and wiry as an Indian's. There always had been something of an Indian about Reeves. His high cheek bones, his spare, expressionless face, his steady stare, his mouth that seldom opened unless he had something important to say were like an Indian's.

In less than a year after Caleb Reeves had first pinned the sheriff's badge on his vest, he had swept lawlessness out of the Pie River country. He had shot men, brought men in to be tried and hung, and followed relentlessly with his hard-riding posses after men who kept going, and stayed away from the Pie River country if they were lucky enough to escape. Caleb Reeves hated an outlaw.

Steve had heard as a boy, and never had reason to doubt, that Caleb Reeves found more joy in killing or hanging an outlaw than in anything else life offered him. He was a bitter man, Caleb Reeves, and his bitterness was savage against those who followed the outlaw trails.

A gnarled thumb crooked tautly about the lifted hammer of the old single-action gun boring into Steve's middle. A slight shift of the thumb, the space of a breath, and it would be over. Steve felt his stomach muscles tightening, crawling.

Gray streaked the sheriff's temples now; his lean face had grown thinner with the passing years, so that his hooked nose stood out more fiercely than ever. Wrinkles were beginning to trough his leathered cheeks. But his hand was as steady; his eyes were clear and chill; the gun was no less deadly.

Steve said again evenly: "You can't scare me, Reeves. I haven't got anything to tell you. If you're looking for some excuse to let that hammer drop, fish it out. The deal is yours."

Steve recognized the scowling young man who rolled a cigarette, struck a match, made a comment with a sneer. "Put a rope over one of those piñon limbs outside, Sheriff, an' stretch his neck a little. Maybe it'll help his memory."

That was Buster Davis, whose father had run the hardware store. Buster still had the scar under his ear where the wall-eyed filly had thrown him when he was eleven. Even then Buster had been a surly, sneering boy, ready to bully when he could.

Steve grinned coldly. "Buster, you must be remembering the time I punched the stuffing out of you and made you cry . . . 'yellow' . . . back of the harness shop."

"You lied as quick then as you do now," Buster Davis snapped.

The sheriff jerked his head impatiently. "Never mind talkin' over old times. Three days ago, mister, you was seen over near Jawbone Mountain with a man who held up the stage a couple of years back. His mask slipped then, an' he was seen plain by Henry Simpson here. I trailed him for a couple of days before he shook us off. Now I aim to get him. We trailed you both from Jawbone Mountain to this neck of the woods. Now where's your sidekick?"

"I told you," said Steve, "you're talking Apache. I don't savvy. You can gouge that cannon up under my liver and pull the trigger and I still won't savvy. That plain?"

"Too damned plain," said Caleb Reeves harshly. "You're coverin' this jasper up. You know where he is."

"Why don't you look around?" suggested Steve. "Maybe he's hiding under that old windmill, or laying up on the roof, laughing at you."

The gun gouged deeper. "Your ideas," said Caleb Reeves coldly, "don't help you none."

"You men come busting in here," said Steve to them, "waving your guns under my nose and shouting questions. Which is not the way to make me remember anything. Maybe I did meet up with a stranger. I meet plenty of strangers. But I haven't been in these parts for twelve years. I didn't know you were looking for anybody. I'm not one of your deputies. I'm not interested in Pie River law. I aimed to camp here for a day or so and mind my own business, while trying to decide what to do now that I'm back home. And you bust in on me, demanding answers. You'll get the same answer if you stay till the desert gets blizzards. I'm no outlaw. I'm not interested in outlaws. I haven't any idea where this *hombre* is you're looking for. Now what are you going to do about it?"

Buster Davis snapped: "Buzzards always hang together!"

"If that was always the case," said Steve, "you'd be on your belly with the other snakes."

"Never mind jawin' at each other," said Caleb Reeves impatiently. "What are you doin' back in these parts?"

"Looking around," said Steve.

"What for?"

"I thought I might buy me a piece of land and settle down. I'm tired of sloping."

"It takes money to buy land."

"I've got money."

"Where'd you get it?"

"Gold mining down in Mexico, if you've got to be so damned curious."

"You made money minin' gold over the border," said Reeves with cold suspicion. "And now you're comin' back to ranch when everybody's losin' money at it. It don't make sense."

"Who said it made sense?" said Steve calmly. "I left a heap of friends in these parts when I went away as a kid. When I figured to settle down, I thought of home. Maybe it doesn't make sense, but it was good enough for me. Now I don't know. If a bull-headed old gunslinger and this hot-headed posse are a sample of the rest of the Pie River country nowadays, maybe I was fool to come back. I used to think you was some shucks as a sheriff. You're acting like a boogery steer now. You've been wearing a badge too long. And make up you're mind what you aim to do about me. My arms are getting tired."

Caleb Reeves caught an end of his brown-stained mustache in a corner of his mouth and stared. His eyes were frosty blue, gunman's eyes. Looking at the seamed, hard face, Steve knew that here was a man. Bitter, hard, ruthless, Reeves might be, but he'd never run from a gun, never turn his back on danger or a bluff.

"I remember you," Reeves said. "I remember your old man. Pete Cochrane was all right. You have good blood in you."

"Never mind my blood," said Steve. "I'm asking you for a showdown."

"If I thought you was an outlaw," said Reeves, "I'd settle your hash quick. But I ain't sure, and I never aim to go off half-cocked."

Two men stepped in from outside.

"Any signs of the other one?" asked Reeves.

"Tracks around the corral," was the answer.

"Reckon he's gone on, then?"

"Looks like it."

Caleb Reeves looked at Steve's blanket roll in the corner, glanced at the rifle leaning beside the door, let his frosty blue eyes wander around the room.

"No sign in here," said Reeves. He shrugged and slowly holstered his gun. "Take down your hands," he told Steve. "Looks like you're tellin' the truth. I hope so, for your sake. If I ketch you with that damned outlaw, or find you mixed up in any crooked business on this range, I'll ride you twice as hard. It don't set kindly with me to have an owl-hoot buzzard make

139

a monkey outta me."

Steve lowered his arms, stretched them, grinned thinly. "Thanks for nothing. And now, I'll tell you all something. I don't take kindly to being spied on. If I start rambling around looking for a piece of land to buy, I don't want any rannies fogging my trail back where their dust hangs low. Give me my gun and make yourselves at home or drift on. It's all the same."

"Give him his gun," said Caleb Reeves.

The long-waisted cowman at the sheriff's right surrendered Steve's six-gun in silence.

Reeves's cold blue eyes rested on Steve for a moment, while the possemen drifted toward the door.

"I don't know what to make of you," said Reeves. "You talk big." Reeves fingered his mustache, shrugged, and decided. "If you stay around, I'll make up my mind."

The sheriff strode out. Buster Davis let Steve see his scowl before leaving.

In the doorway Steve watched them fork leather and gallop down the slope, across the dry wash and up the other slope into the piñons. When the last man was gone and the noise of their passing had died away, Steve kicked viciously at a rusty sardine tin, and bitterly addressed a buzzard wheeling in slow circles over the piñons behind the cabin.

"Why in hell did something like this have to happen?" he asked bitterly. "Now I've got to stick my head in a noose, or figure myself a skunk. I might have known better than to come back this way."

II

"BROTHER JACK"

Costerville lay in the southeast, where the flood-scoured channel of Hatchet Creek came out of the gullied foothills. Steve rode into the northeast, leading the gray pack mare.

The sun was dropping to the jagged crest of the Jawbone Range, some forty miles across the lowlands. Steve rode leisurely through the piñon ridges. Now and then he watched behind. Once he tied the pack mare and circled back to watch the back trail in the fast-fading light. No one seemed to be following.

Miles north of Costerville, where the road began a tortuous climb to the rimrock above, and Paloma Creek came tumbling out of a narrow, rocky cañon, there was a rambling log building backed by corrals and two open-front sheds. A crudely lettered sign over the door said: **Brother Jack, Eats.**

Steve remembered the place. A Mexican had owned it years back, and the Mexican's father before him. Travelers off the rimrock, heading toward Costerville, usually stopped to fill their belts. Going the other way, travelers were glad to stop before making the hard climb to the rimrock and the dry *malpais* country to the north.

Tonight the moon was not yet up over the rimrock when Steve dropped stiffly out of the saddle and tied his horses to the sagging hitch rail. A buggy, two wagons, half a dozen saddled horses were already at the hitch rail. Loud laughter and talk came through the open door. Tall and stringy, Steve had to stoop when he passed through the door. He squinted against the light and looked around the small, low-ceilinged room.

A man in old sheepskin chaps was tilted back against the wall in a chair held together by wire. He lowered a crumpled newspaper and stared as the stranger entered. On the wall over his head was tacked a yellowed piece of cardboard crudely lettered in red paint.

WELCOME BROTHER, SIN NOT

Other signs were on the log walls.

**PEACE TO ALL
REST WITH BROTHER JACK
FRIENDS BE FRIENDS IN HERE
NO CUSSIN', PLEASE**

Other men were clustered at a plank bar across one end of the room, with whisky glasses and beer bottles before them.

A pretty, black-eyed Mexican girl collecting soiled dishes from a table paused and eyed Steve with approval as he went to the bar.

"Howdy, men," Steve said.

They nodded. One or two greeted him. He spoke to the tall, bearded man behind the bar.

"Got another bottle of beer, mister?"

"Brother, I got a barrel full of bottles," was the sonorous reply. "Here's one that just come up outta the crick. It's good an' cold."

Steve set down the foam-wet bottle half empty and grinned. "That lays the dust where it's needed."

The man at Steve's right, broad-shouldered, powerful, young-looking despite his square-cut, reddish beard, commented: "You look like you been travelin' through plenty of dust. Come off the *malpais?*"

"Nope, I cut across by Jawbone Mountain."

"Plenty dusty over that way, eh?"

"Plenty."

Brother Jack, behind the bar, rested two big gnarled hands on the age-blackened planks. An old man, Brother Jack was still huge despite the stoop bowing his powerful shoulders. The bushy beard that covered his face and fell down over his chest was dirty white, and the beard grew up past his ears and high up on his cheeks. A drooping mustache hid his mouth. Bushy eyebrows tangled on jutting eye ridges under which large, unwinking eyes stared mildly. Above the bulging forehead there was no hair, only a polished, leather-colored dome that gleamed in the lamplight. That high, polished skull above the white beard gave Brother Jack a commanding, patriarchal look, and his deep, slow voice seemed to come from a chest that had no bottom.

He said mildly: "Jawbone Mountain's kinda off the trails around here, brother. You must've come up from the border."

"I've been down thataway," Steve admitted.

"Ridin' on north?"

"I'm ridin' ham an' eggs an' fried spuds an' coffee, if you got 'em."

Brother Jack nodded. "Josita!" he called. "Tell your old lady to hot up some ham an' fixin's."

"*Sí, señor,*" answered Josita meekly. She vanished into a back kitchen with the wet rag she had been using on the table.

Steve ate ravenously, trading smiles with the saucy-eyed Josita who hovered near the table for a time.

Two of the customers went out, and a wagon rattled away. The man with the reddish beard leaned over the end of the bar and talked to Brother Jack in an undertone. From the corner of his eye, Steve caught them both looking at him. Presently the red-bearded man walked out and the pound of his galloping horse vanished in the night.

Brother Jack lifted the hinged end of the counter and came to the table. "Grub all right, brother?" he inquired.

"Suits me," said Steve, putting down the tin cup of coffee.

"Ridin' on tonight?"

"That depends," said Steve. "I'm looking for a friend of mine who came this way."

Brother Jack stroked his beard. "Lots of folks come this way. Maybe he'll be along tonight. What's his name?"

"Smoky Davis," said Steve, dropping his voice.

For an instant the huge, gnarled hand paused on the dirty white beard. Then the fingers combed gently in, and the leathery dome of Brother Jack's skull caught the lamplight as he shook his head. "Don't know the fellow," he stated mildly.

"Didn't say you did," said Steve casually as he scraped a piece of bread around on the plate. "I reckon he's been here, if somebody ain't put a bullet in him, and that isn't too likely. He's a short fellow, good-looking, talks quiet and soft. Riding a roan with a white blaze on its nose."

"Friend, you say, brother?"

Steve nodded.

"How long have you known him?"

"Long enough."

"Long enough for what, brother?"

"Long enough to be looking for him," said Steve calmly.

Brother Jack sat down at the side of the table and smoothed his beard tranquilly. "You sure this here friend of yourn was by here, brother?"

"Smoky started here an' I reckon he got here," said Steve, reaching for the tobacco bag in his shirt pocket. "Smoky's

144

that kind of a fellow."

"If he shows up," said Brother Jack, "I'll tell him you were here."

Steve flipped a match alight. "It might be better, brother," he suggested, "if you tell me where Smoky is now. I've got business with Smoky, and I don't aim to be put off by any psalm-talking mossy-horn with a mattress on his face. Do you follow me, brother?"

Brother Jack combed his beard with his fingers. His chest lifted in a sigh. "Son," he muttered, "when I was a young 'un, I didn't like talk like that."

"I reckon you don't like it now," said Steve. "Where's Smoky?"

"I told you. . . ."

"Never mind telling me again." Steve leaned forward, speaking calmly under his breath. "Smoky told me he knew you from away back. Never mind heaving dust in my face. It don't matter a damn to me why you're covering up for Smoky, but I aim to see him."

"Brother, I'm an old man. . . ."

"You'll be a damn' sight older when I get through with you, if you don't come through about Smoky," said Steve evenly.

"That ain't no way to talk to me, brother."

Brother Jack's big, gnarled hand smoothed the under side of his beard, and flicked out and rested on the table. All but concealed under the gnarled fingers was a runty little double-barreled Derringer that had come from some hiding spot under the beard. Brother Jack said apologetically: "There's times I forget myself. I'm only a pore sinner, but I don't take to bein' backed in a corner when I'm tryin' to do my best."

Steve grinned. "Brother Jack," he said, "you have converted me. The pot is yours, an' now what?"

"Son," said Brother Jack, putting both elbows on the table and dropping his other hand over the Derringer, "you talk reasonable. I find myself likin' you and forgivin' your hasty ways. If you're a friend of Smoky Davis's, you're a friend of mine. That's from the heart, brother, from the heart of Brother Jack."

"Brother Jack," said Steve, "you move me deeply. But where in hell is Smoky?"

There was a call from the bar. "More beer, Jack!"

Brother Jack's deep voice bellowed from the depths of his beard, while his eyes stayed on Steve's face. "Gregorio! Tend bar, I'm busy right now!"

The stolid young man who came from the back of the building was hardly more than a boy, a year or so older than the pretty Josita, and somewhat of a dandy, with his grease-slicked black hair, tight trousers, and a gaily embroidered vest. Steve wondered about him and the pretty Mexican girl, and the mother who was back there in the kitchen. Were they the Mexican family that had lived here in years past? And if they were, how did Brother Jack happen to be running the place?

At the moment that didn't matter. Brother Jack was speaking softly in his beard: "Your friend Smoky was here. But he's gone. I don't look for him back."

"Where'd he go?"

"Are you sure it's important, brother?"

"Plenty important."

"It's a right smart ride to where Smoky is," said Brother Jack reflectively. "I ain't sure he'll be there when you get there. But I'll tell you, son, an' hope for the best. I'll have to draw you a map. It's over by Lariat Cañon, on the edge of the *malpais* back of Costerville."

"I know the place," said Steve.

146

Brother Jack's heavy eyebrows lifted. "You live around here?"

"I used to, when I was a kid."

"You ain't been around here lately, I take it. I've never seen you before."

"That's right," said Steve.

"You know how to get there," said Brother Jack. "Go to Lariat Cañon, where the Twin Rocks is. A couple of miles up, there's a little side cañon. Smoky oughta be camped there."

"What's he doing there?"

"Smoky didn't tell me his plans, son," said Brother Jack mildly. "That's all I can do for you. Step up to the bar an' have a bottle of beer. You got plenty of time to be ridin' yet. The grub is on me, too, brother. I like your style."

The Mexican boy vanished into the kitchen. While Steve was drinking the beer, Brother Jack walked back there, too. He returned with a paper-wrapped package.

"Here's some grub for you, son. You might get hungry 'long about midnight."

Steve stacked two silver dollars on the counter. "No offense meant for refusing the treat. Thanks for the grub. It's more'n I expected. *Adiós.*"

Brother Jack lifted his hand in a gesture that was almost a benediction. "Good bye, brother," he said sonorously. "A pleasant ride to you."

Steve went out, puzzled. There was a queer character. Smoky Davis had been vague about Brother Jack. One thing was certain, despite his meekness, the old man could take care of himself. What was Smoky doing up Lariat Cañon? Why had he pushed on alone, apologetically, as if no business was more important than a visit to Brother Jack?

Steve had the lead rope and the reins of the sorrel in one hand and was reaching for the stirrup with the other when a whisper came out of the night behind him.

"*¡Señor!*"

She was a slim, vague figure in the moonlight, wary, frightened. She watched the open door fearfully as she stepped close.

"What is it?" Steve asked under his breath.

"*Señor,* don' go, don' go!"

"Why not?"

"Gregorio, hees ride ahead."

"Gregorio gone to the cañon?"

"*Sí.*"

"Why?"

"They keel you, *señor.*"

"Who'll kill me?"

"*Señor,* don' go! An' eef you see thees Smoky, tell heem Josita thanks him."

She was gone, a flitting, silent shadow, back behind the building.

Steve swore softly, hesitated, half minded to return to the bar. But that would mean trouble for the girl. He rode off, testing his belt gun and the rifle in the saddle boot by his leg.

III

"DRY-GULCHER'S PAY-OFF"

The Twin Rocks were slender spires where the weather-gutted, eroded *malpais* land dropped down into Lariat Cañon. Under the full moon the rocks were visible long before Steve reached them. They were a landmark. A rough trail dropped down at that point into the cañon.

Before riding down, Steve turned in the saddle and looked off into the southwest. Those faint lights on the lower lands were Costerville, seven or eight miles away. Costerville, on Hatchet Creek. This was a strange place for Smoky Davis to be. Up Lariat Cañon was nothing.

It was also strange that Smoky Davis had gone to see Brother Jack. It was strange that Smoky had ridden on to this bleak, deserted cañon above Costerville. And there was the warning of Josita. Her voice had trembled with earnestness. She had believed she was telling the truth. But she was hardly more than a kid, and Smoky Davis had proved himself in the past. There'd be no dry-gulching of Steve Cochrane while Smoky Davis was near.

Brother Jack evidently didn't know that. He had played his cards wrong. Smiling thinly, Steve led the pack mare down the rough trail to the cañon floor, along which a tumbling thread of water burbled snake-like. In the black shadows and quiet, the shod hoofs of the horses rang loudly. But Smoky would be expecting him.

Steve knew the cañon, knew every mile of this country, and it seemed to him that the ghost of another rider kept pace up the cañon, a barefoot boy on a bareback pony, eagerly exploring here on the fringe of the *malpais*.

Then the narrow mouth of the pocket cañon yawned just ahead on the right. When Steve came opposite, he saw the wink of a fire back in a rock-walled pocket hardly more than an acre in size. Back in there were horses, half a dozen at least, picketed near the fire. Their heads lifted, ears pricked toward Steve. But no men were visible.

"Smoky!" Steve called.

His answer was a crashing gunshot from the rocky slope behind him. A cold flick against his left arm was followed by a loud whinny of pain from the gray pack mare as she staggered and tore the lead rope out of Steve's fingers. The pack mare had walked up abreast when Steve had stopped. She was between Steve and the little side cañon, and Steve was between the mare and the gunman or gunmen behind him. The bullet had gouged Steve's arm, traveled on downward, and struck the mare high in the neck, near the skull. She staggered, lurched to her knees, rolled on her side, kicking. Steve barely saw that as the sorrel leaped ahead under slashing spurs.

Josita had been right. This was death, death from behind, grimly without warning. And if Smoky had a hand in it, there was no trust and honor to friendship, no one to whom any man could turn for safety.

The pack mare had fallen inside the belt of shadow near the cañon wall. Steve was out in the white, flooding moonlight. He yanked the sorrel toward that shadow belt as he bolted up the cañon. If Smoky and the other riders from those picketed horses were ambushed up in the rocks, their guns would be reaching for him.

A second bullet struck the sorrel as Steve heard the whip-like crack of the shot. The sorrel plunged down, too. Steve kicked his feet from the stirrups, snatched for the rifle as he launched himself from the saddle. He landed in a staggering, stumbling run, the rifle muzzle trailing in the sand behind. Instinctively he gripped the smooth wooden stock hard. Without the rifle, and afoot, he had no chance.

The sorrel rolled heavily on the sand and rocks. Here the cañon wall was sheer. There was no cover. Steve spun around in a dodging crouch, shaking the rifle to clear any sand from the muzzle.

Sparks flew as the sorrel kicked against small boulders. A third rifle shot drove a bullet smashing into the rocky wall behind Steve. A wet, gurgling sound came from the sorrel's mouth. It died there, and lay still with blood gushing from its nostrils. Steve threw himself down behind the sorrel.

The mare was still kicking, trying to get up. But she was dying, too. A fourth shot thudded hollowly into the sorrel's belly. Steve caught a saddle string and pushed it into the rifle muzzle to make sure no clogging sand would split the barrel wide.

The barrel was clear. He pumped a shell into the breech. His eyes were narrowed, calculating. No storm of lead, no fusillade of shots had come from that nest of rocks across the cañon. Four shots only, spaced close together, in the time a fast-shooting man might lever shells into his rifle and throw down in quick aim.

One man! If more men were up there, they would have been shooting by now. No matter where the other men were. They might be coming fast, might be closing in from both sides. But at the moment, one man!

Steve peered cautiously past the saddle. The moonlight played on the rocks where the lone gunman hid. He must have counted on dropping his victim with the first shot. Now he was trapped up there himself, couldn't go up or down or show himself.

A fifth shot blasted, and Steve saw the wink of light low down between two big boulders, and he knew where his man was, and it was an easy shot. Steve sighted carefully. The other man would be straining his eyes, getting ready for another shot, would be exposing himself between those two boulders, not sure whether his victim was down for good or not.

Steve squeezed the trigger before the sixth shot came, before the man had time to dodge back to safety. He fired low, where the crouching figure of a peering man would be. There was no cry of pain. Steve fancied he saw a flurry of movement back of the boulders, thought he heard metal strike against rock. Then the silence of death fell over the cañon. Even the gray mare lay quietly now.

He waited, and it seemed that the slow, hard beats of his heart must be audible. The sixth shot did not come. The quiet seemed to press down like a heavy weight. Then a grating cry rang out with uncanny clearness.

"I'm dyin'! Do somethin' for me!"

"You asked for it!" Steve called. "Don't think I'm damned fool enough to walk out there and get potted!"

The man strangled, coughed audibly. "I'm holed, I tell you!"

"Crawl out in the open if you're that bad, you snake!" Steve ordered.

"I cain't move!"

But the stranger did move, with a flopping, twisting motion that brought his body out into view beside a boulder. He slipped, fell, rolled down in plain sight before another rock stopped him.

"Don't move!" Steve called.

He ran across the cañon, rifle cocked, ready, and climbed up the slope. Before he reached the prone figure, he knew this was no trickery. The man was strangling again when Steve bent over him. Dark blood was on his lips in the moonlight. He was half doubled up, clutching his middle.

"I'm all tore up inside!" he gasped. "In my belly an' chest!"

His mustache was black, and he wore rawhide chaps and a leather vest, and a stubble of black beard covered his thin face. His eyes seemed to bulge in a frightened stare as the moonlight struck against them.

"Lemme see," said Steve.

The bullet had struck the gun belt buckle and ranged up through the stomach, probably into the chest. Men did not get well from wounds like this.

"You fixed me, didn't you, fella?"

"I reckon so," agreed Steve heavily. Regret made him gruff. "Why'n hell did you dry-gulch me that way?"

The wounded man did not answer.

"That Mex boy brought word from Brother Jack I was coming, didn't he?"

The man nodded, groaned: "I should've told that Mex to go to hell. I might've known it was bad luck to drop a stranger like that."

"Why'd you want to kill me?"

The answer was surprising. "Damned if I know. You was bringin' trouble, the Mex kid said."

"I was lookin' for Smoky Davis."

"He ain't here."

"Where'd he go?"

Blood was getting in the throat, choking, cutting off air from the chest. The man got his throat clear and lay panting for a moment.

"All I want is to find Smoky Davis," said Steve.

"He's in town."

"Costerville?"

"Yep."

"What's he doin' there?"

"He's with the boys."

"What boys?"

"Hell, stranger," was the weak counter, "doncha know nothin'?"

"I'm Smoky Davis's pardner, that's all I know."

"He's in Costerville." The man began to choke again.

Steve waited. "Who else is around here?" he questioned, after a moment.

"Nobody."

Steve had to bend close to hear that hoarse, labored whisper. It didn't make sense.

"What's Smoky doing in Costerville? When's he coming back out here?"

The wounded man was gasping, rattling in his throat. He turned half over, leaned back, seemed to relax peacefully. When Steve lifted one of the bloody hands, it came limply, and fell soggily.

Steve's arm was bleeding slowly. The wound wasn't deep. He rolled up the shirt sleeve, tied his bandanna over the furrow, rolled down the sleeve again, and put on his coat. With a little effort he got the saddle off the dead sorrel. The gray mare and the pack would have to stay here. The picketed horses in the little pocket cañon eyed him curiously as he lugged the saddle to them. One already was saddled.

Steve picked out a powerful black horse and cinched on the saddle. The horse might have been rustled, might be recognized by an owner in Costerville, but the risk had to be faced. The black was fresh, full of fire. Steve let him have his head down the cañon, away from that place of death.

IV

"LARIAT CAÑON"

Costerville had grown larger, but the same main street was there, with the small brick courthouse and jail under the cottonwoods at one end. The church had a new coat of paint and a spire. There were more houses and stores and saloons than Steve recalled. Now, an hour and a half before midnight, hitch racks still were full; stores were open for business. Steve remembered, then, that this was Saturday night. The town would be awake until well after midnight.

He rode the length of the street, and saw no sign of Smoky. He hitched the horse at one of the courthouse racks and started back afoot to search saloons and stores. He was wary, tense as he went. That furtive signal that had gone on ahead to ambush and kill him was warning enough that Smoky was flirting with trouble.

Ten minutes later Steve stepped out of Thad Stephens's General Store. Caleb Reeves, the sheriff, was waiting on the walk, thumbs hooked in his gun belt, and a stony, suspicious look was on his seamed face.

"So you're in town now?" said the sheriff.

"Your eyes are right," said Steve.

"One of the boys said he seen you down the street. You seem to be lookin' for something."

"The last time I saw this street," said Steve, "I was only a kid. Tonight, I'm taking a good look again."

Reeves bent closer. "That a bullet hole in your coat sleeve?"

The blood had not soaked through. The bandanna underneath was holding it in now. "That's a bullet hole," Steve admitted. "Someday I'll have it patched."

"Where'd you get it?"

"Ever hear of Torquemado?"

"Nope," denied Reeves suspiciously.

"Then there isn't any use tellin' you," said Steve calmly. "Too bad I wasn't wearin' this coat when your posse jumped me. You could have asked more questions."

Reeves chewed the end of his tobacco-stained mustache, frowning under the broad hat brim. "I still ain't made up my mind about you, Cochrane. But it don't set too well to see you here in Costerville. Some buzzards are evidently figurin' I'm too old to back up a sheriff's badge an' are hornin' in on this range. I'm proddy about it, Cochrane."

Steve grinned thinly. He was as tall as the sheriff, so that their eyes were level. They faced each other across a gulf of years, with a wariness that had all the tension of cocked triggers.

"You always were proddy about outlaws," said Steve.

"I always will be, mister." Reeves clenched a fist. His voice grew harsh. "I'm livin' to get all the outlaws I can while I'm alive. Remember that, Cochrane, while I'm makin' up my mind about you."

"You make it plain, anyway," said Steve. "Have you found your man from Jawbone Mountain?"

"If he stays on the Pie River range, I'll get him," promised Reeves. "An' I'll bring him back in a wagon with his boots on. Watch your step, Cochrane."

Caleb Reeves strode away, a tall, wiry, bitter man. Steve searched again, listening for an eruption of gunfire. If Smoky was in town and was recognized, gun play would follow.

More than one face was familiar, but Steve was not the boy who had left Costerville. No one recognized him.

A man with a square-cut, reddish beard walked diagonally across the dusty street. Steve watched him enter the liveliest saloon on the other side of the street. Years ago the spot had been a vacant lot. Steve crossed the street, also. That square-cut reddish beard had leaned over Brother Jack's dirty bar in low-voiced conversation with Brother Jack.

The Stag Bar was still busy, despite the late hour and riders and wagons and buggies leaving town. The bar sign was lettered: **R. B. Davis, Prop.** Steve was in the swinging doors before the name struck him. Robert Davis had been the school name of Buster Davis.

The reddish-bearded stranger was ordering a drink. He saw Steve's reflection in the bar mirror and turned. Their eyes met. The red-bearded man flicked a glance to the rear of the room, and back to Steve. His teeth showed.

"Have a drink, mister?"

"Thank you, no."

At one of the back tables Smoky was sitting, face to the door, unconcernedly finishing a game of solitaire. Two empty beer bottles were at his elbow. Smoky looked up as Steve reached the table. Smoky's lean, cheerful face was blank. He gave no sign of recognition as he scooped up the cards and began to riffle the deck.

"Get the hell outta here," Smoky said when Steve sat down.

"You damned idjit," said Steve under his breath. "*You* get out of town. There's a pack of trouble pilin' up for you."

Smoky did not look up. "Don't be seen talking to me. I'm bad medicine tonight, Steve."

"You don't have to tell me," said Steve. "I was looking for you up at Brother Jack's place. He sent me on to Lariat Cañon and sent word ahead to put a bullet in me. I killed the fellow who laid for me."

Smoky cut the cards, stacked them again, and started to deal a new lay-out. "You kilt him?"

"He opened up on me from behind. Nicked my arm and got both my horses."

"Anybody else up there in the cañon now?"

"Hell's fire, no. Didn't you hear me say one of your friends opened up at my back with a gun? What kind of business is this?"

"Keep your voice down," warned Smoky. His own voice was strained, wooden. Smoky looked different. His face might have been cut from a block of stone.

157

"Are you tied up with that red-bearded gent at the bar?"

"Plenty," said Smoky, hardly moving his lips.

"And with this Brother Jack?"

"You might say so."

"And you're sitting there, not batting an eye when I tell you what happened?"

"Will you hightail out of here?" said Smoky through his teeth. "Someday I'll tell you all about it."

Steve felt the blood pounding in his temples as anger grew hot and strong inside. "Listen, Smoky, we've been pardners. You saved my life down on the border. I owe you plenty for it. We were aiming to drift in here and buy us a ranch and settle down."

"Tell me about it later," said Smoky in the strange, flat voice. Little drops of perspiration were appearing on Smoky's forehead.

"This afternoon," said Steve, "a sheriff's posse jumped me at that adobe shack. They were looking for you. That man we met over by Jawbone Mountain a couple of days ago spotted you as the one who held up the stage here a couple of years ago. I talked 'em off, and rode to this Brother Jack's where you said you were going. The stage didn't matter to me. I took you as you were since we met up. I tried to find you and warn you to get going before a posse gives you noose law. And all I got was a bullet at my back and you trying to run me out now. What are you up to, Smoky? The sheriff has halfway decided I'm an outlaw. If I'm going to have the name, I'm going to know what's behind it."

Smoky looked past Steve, to the bar. A low groan of helplessness burst from him, and he dropped the cards, pushed back the chair, stood up, and his hand was on the gun at his side.

"I didn't want this to happen!" husked Smoky. "Stand

back, Steve. Hell is due to pop."

Smoky's eyes were on the bar. Steve turned, taut with apprehension at what he saw on Smoky's face. He hadn't seen Buster Davis come in. But Buster was there behind the bar, at the back, where the gold-scrolled door of a massive iron safe stood ajar. The red-bearded man, and two other men among the customers whom Steve had not noticed, had stepped back into the clear with drawn guns.

The red-bearded man barked a preëmptory order: "Lift 'em, boys, an' you won't get hurt!"

Buster Davis made the mistake of trying to dodge down behind the bar. Smoky's gun roared. Buster staggered against the back-bar, his shoulder drooping queerly, while Smoky jumped toward the safe.

"Smoky!" Steve called involuntarily.

The red-bearded man swung on him with quick fury. "Do I have to drop you?"

"Lay off him, Red!" Smoky gritted. "He's with me!"

"Why'n hell didn't you say so? Tell him to get his gun out an' get to work!"

The swinging doors burst open. One of the townsmen looked in to see what the shooting was about. A bullet drove him tumbling back outside. Steve hardly saw it. He was looking at the sneering fury on Buster Davis's face. Buster spoke to him across the bar, while the echo of the shot was still ringing in their ears.

"I knew you was a damned outlaw! Too bad we didn't string you up this afternoon! But we'll get you!"

"Shut up!" Smoky threw over his shoulder.

Smoky had jerked the safe door wide, was clawing open the inner door. From under his shirt he took a stout cloth sack. In it he dropped a money bag that lay on the floor, and he swept in gold and bills and silver stacked inside the safe. It took only seconds, and in that time shouts were rising outside. The red-bearded man and his men were edging toward the back of the room, watching the door.

"Come on Steve!" rapped Smoky.

Steve drew his gun with a bitter, crooked smile at this twist of fate. Gun killings were not new; hold-ups he had seen; he had traded shot for shot with men who laughed at death. But this had the harsh mirth of a cruel joke. In sixty seconds, against his will and knowledge, he had been turned into an outlaw. Smoky had tried to stop him. Smoky had tried to explain, and the swift-rushing tide of carefully planned action had engulfed them both. Now it was: take it outlaw style or hang.

Two swift shots sounded back of the building.

"Make it fast!" rapped Smoky coolly.

Steve followed him through a narrow hall to the back door. The other three gunmen backed after them.

A sharp voice addressed Smoky as he reached the night: "They're comin'!"

A rider was holding four saddled horses. Smoky turned his head. "Where's your horse, Steve?"

"In front of the courthouse!"

"Hit it behind me!"

Tumult broke out in the saloon as the three gunmen ran out and dived for their horses.

Around the corner of the building a harsh familiar voice shouted: "They're back here, boys!"

That was Caleb Reeves. As they thundered off in the moonlight along the alley behind the buildings, Steve glimpsed the old sheriff's tall figure backing the blistering streaks of a blasting gun. Roaring guns from the flying saddles did not stop him. One of the outlaws pitched to the ground.

"Leave him there!" Smoky yelled. "They'll be down on us

like hornets in a minute!"

Smoky led the retreat around in front of the courthouse. Here was quiet, peace for a moment as Smoky jerked his horse into a rearing stop. Steve flung himself toward his horse, tore the reins from the hitch rack, and hit the leather as the horse bolted forward. He was thundering up beside Smoky a moment later, and the retreat swept on out of town. Behind them men were shouting; guns were firing; horses were drumming as the first hasty pursuit gathered and roared after them.

They headed toward Lariat Cañon, toward the *malpais* country, the foothills, the mountains on beyond. And the pace was killing. No horse could stand this thundering, breakneck speed for long. The Costerville men seemed to realize it; they saved their horses, dropping farther behind. Their riding had a careful grim tenacity.

But they didn't know about those fresh, strong mounts picketed in Lariat Cañon. They didn't know this killing ride to the cañon would put the outlaws on fresh horses that could draw away with ease. And it happened that way.

The fire in the little side cañon had burned down to a few red coals. The dead pack mare and the dead sorrel were there on the rocks, and only the dead man's silent eyes watched the quick shifting of saddles and a fresh leg of the retreat begun. Smoky curtly explained the dead horses and missing guard.

"Joe tangled with my pardner here. He's dead. Forget about him."

The red-bearded man was the only one who made a comment. "Your friend seems to be in it every way we turn."

"Which is my business, Red!" retorted Smoky coldly. "I'm givin' orders till the pay-off. Shut up!"

Still ahead of the pursuit they rode easily up Lariat Cañon. The cañon floor mounted steadily, and presently the walls grew lower, and after a time they were out in the full moonlight that spread over the gullied, eroded, tortuous *malpais* sweep.

Smoky drew rein on a low ridge from which they could see in all directions.

"There's enough moonlight to see," said Smoky. "We'll split here an' scatter."

A coat was spread on the ground. The bag was emptied on it. A hasty count and division were made. There was over six thousand dollars.

"That Davis fellow," explained Smoky to Steve, "owns a big general store down the street, an' another saloon where there's gamblin'. Folks leave money in his safe until the bank opens on Monday morning. He's had a habit of pickin' up the last money an' puttin' it in his safe just about the time he did tonight. He's been askin' for a hold-up. They've got too used to dependin' on that prod-headed old sheriff."

"You planned everything out pat," Steve commented colorlessly.

"Yeah," agreed Smoky, counting money swiftly. "Two of the boys are dead. That leaves four piles. Here's yours, Red. Lefty, there you are. We'll scatter out from here. It's every *hombre* for himself."

The red-bearded man stuffed handfuls of coins and bills in his coat pocket. "I'll string along with you," he decided. "I'm goin' the same place you are."

"Your mistake," refused Smoky. "We're splittin' up."

"I told Jack I'd come in with you."

"You mean Jack told you to stick close to me," said Smoky, straightening up. "He's so crooked he can't trust himself, but I'm tellin' you what to do."

"Have it your own way," was the sulky reply.

V
"OWLHOOT MAVERICK"

They split up there, fanning out in different directions without farewells. Smoky sat in the saddle till the red-bearded man was beyond sight, and then grunted to himself as he lifted the reins and rode off.

"That Denver Red is a mean one," said Smoky.

Steve said nothing.

Smoky looked across in the moonlight. "Sorta feelin' that way about me, ain't you, Steve?"

"No," denied Steve. "I reckon you know what you're doing. When I take a man for a pardner, I take him for bad and good. And you saved my life once."

"We're clean on that. Forget it. I reckon we split up now. If you want to cut off on your own from here, it's all right. I'll understand. I owe you plenty of thanks for tryin' to save me from a tight tonight."

"You're still in a tight," said Steve. "Reeves, the sheriff, ain't a man to take his teeth out of a thing like this."

"He's just a sheriff," said Smoky. "I've handled better sheriffs than he'll ever be. Soon as I turn this money over, I'm ridin', an' I won't be back on this range."

"That goes for both of us."

"I'm sorry, Steve. When I was makin' plans with you, I didn't know all this'd break."

"This Brother Jack is behind it?"

"Yes," admitted Smoky glumly. He cursed. "I'd have killed him if it'd done any good. But this was the only way."

163

"You didn't have to do this to get money, Smoky. I had enough to get a small ranch. All you needed to do was tell me you were busted."

"I had money."

"I don't savvy this then."

"You never will understand, I guess," said Smoky heavily. "Steve, we never talked about the past. You never asked me questions."

"The past is your own business."

"It's yours now, I guess," said Smoky. "Steve, this ain't nothin' new to me. I was an outlaw before I met you."

"The sheriff's posse made that plain this afternoon."

"There's a hell of a lot of things they didn't make plain," said Smoky. "It goes away back, Steve, back almost as far as I can remember. I wasn't even five years old when I hit the outlaw trail."

"You started pretty young," Steve remarked dryly.

"I can just remember two folks who must have been my parents," said Smoky. "A woman who held me a lot an' must've loved me a lot. And a big man who used to laugh a heap an' play with me. Sometimes I dream about her, Steve, bendin' over my little bed and smilin' down at me. Hell, Steve, do you remember your mother?"

"Yes," said Steve.

"That's all the memory I've got," said Smoky, and there was a strange, wistful hunger in his voice. "The rest of it starts with a man named Dirk Johnson an' the women at Pyote Springs."

"Never heard of the place."

"You wouldn't," said Smoky. "Strangers weren't welcomed there. It was an outlaw hangout. The women were about what you'd expect. They mothered me a little, when they felt like it, and slapped me around when I got in the way.

Dirk Johnson used to leave me there for long stretches while he was out riding the owlhoot. One woman had been something better than an outlaw's woman, an' she taught me what schoolin' I've had. As soon as I could ride a horse an' hold a gun an' cover country, Dirk Johnson took me out with him and saw to it I finished my schoolin' on the owlhoot."

"A hell of a father," Steve commented.

"He wasn't my father. I didn't know it then. But sometimes he'd stand an' grin at me, nasty-like, as if he was rollin' somethin' over in his mind that pleased him a lot. He had light hair, an' I had dark. We didn't look alike. But I'd been an owlhoot rider for years before I savvied all that. It was natural to me, Steve. I didn't know anything else. You used your brains an' beat the law, an', if you didn't get shot up or caught, everything was all right."

Steve said nothing.

Smoky rode in silence for a few minutes. "Dirk," he said finally, "used to beat me an' act so mean, when he was drunk, I finally cut away from him. I didn't think much more about him until I landed back in Pyote Springs and got to talking to one of the women who was still around. She told me Dirk Johnson wasn't my father. Dirk had boasted of it when he was drunk. She said Dirk an' another man had showed up with me one day an' said I was Dirk's kid, an' nobody asked any questions."

"Looks like Dirk Johnson was a man for you to look up," said Steve slowly.

"I looked him up," said Smoky. "It took me four years to find him." Smoky's voice grew bitter. "And then Dirk was dyin' from knife wounds he got in a drunken fight. I asked him who I was an' where he got me, an' he laughed at me. He knew he was dyin'. There wasn't anything I could do to make him yellow. He told me he'd taken me from my father an' mother for spite, because my mother had married another man an' not him, an' he'd sworn they'd regret it. So he dropped around, when I was only a shaver, an' rode away with me. He said he made an outlaw outta me on purpose. He was laughin' about it when he died. Steve, I don't know what I might've been, instead of an owlhoot rider. All I know is that maybe that woman who smiles down at me in my sleep sometimes, an' that big man who used to pick me up an' play with me, are maybe waitin' around somewheres, wonderin' about me. Like . . . like I wonder about *them*."

In the far distance coyotes were howling mournfully. The moon hung still and white overhead, and Smoky's story suddenly made the night seem empty and lonesome.

Awkwardly Steve said: "Pardner, I'm sorry. What about this other feller?"

"I've been hunting him," said Smoky. "Three years I've been hunting him. At Pyote Springs, he used to call himself Jack Black. He was a bald-headed man. I reckon I've trailed down a thousand bald-headed men, but none of them was Jack Black. Years ago, he was with the Belcher gang for a time, but he left 'em. About two months ago, when we were down in Nogales, I ran across one of the old Pyote Springs men. He said he heard that Jack Black had settled over here in the Pie River country, on the road north of Costerville."

"And was calling himself Brother Jack," Steve supplied.

"That's right," agreed Smoky. "That was when I suggested we ride this way. And the more you talked about settling down, the better I liked the idea . . . after I'd got to Jack Black and heard what he had to tell me. That's why I left you today, Steve, to get Jack Black in a corner an' get the truth outta him."

"What'd he say?"

"He didn't say. I found him there, an' recognized him

behind his beard. He knew me quick enough, too. He'd taken over that place an' married the Mex woman. She'd been right pretty, it seems, before her husband got killed. If you ask me, Jack Black killed him. But that don't matter. There he was, callin' himself Brother Jack, an' he admitted he knew who I was. Said he was with Dirk Johnson when I was taken. An' he offered me a trade. He'd tell me all about it, if I'd help him get this money tonight. He had a hunch this wouldn't go off right unless an old hand like myself was leading the party."

"He must've fooled the sheriff all this time," said Steve.

"I reckon so. Jack Black's been carrying on outlaw business under cover ever since he's been here. The owlhoot knows his place is the right place to stop. But things have been getting a little warm lately. He's ready to quit an' ride on. He needed this money tonight to get away on. So he wouldn't talk unless I helped him out."

"You had a gun, didn't you?"

"He had me hog-tied," said Smoky. "He laughed at me, too. He's the only living man who can tell me what I want to know. I couldn't kill him an' never know."

"I guess so," Steve agreed.

"He offered me a cut," said Smoky. "I turned it down. But I said I'd do the job. One more job wouldn't make much difference, I figured. We could get us a ranch somewhere else. So I've done it, an' I'm takin' Jack Black's money to him an' getting my answer. I reckon it'd've been all right if you hadn't showed up."

"After you get your answer," said Steve grimly, "I'll stay behind and see Jack Black myself. He played his cards wrong with me. The Mexicans won't be too sorry at what happens, I guess."

"I reckon not," agreed Smoky. "He don't treat 'em too well. There's a pretty girl there, Josita, who's scared to death of him. He aimed a lick at her while we were talking in the back room, an' I knocked his hand up."

"She didn't forget it," Steve remembered. "And Smoky, I'm wishing you luck in what he tells you. I hope that . . . that woman you remember is there waiting for you."

"I'm afraid to hope," confessed Smoky. "It's been a long time. But at least I'll know. It won't be eating down inside day an' night."

"We'd better ride along," suggested Steve. "This Denver Red'll get there with his story about me."

"I think Jack Black an' Denver Red are figuring on pullin' out together. We'll beat Red there," said Smoky, spurring.

VI

"AN OUTLAW'S BARGAIN"

The moon was a great silvery disk that flooded cold light over the night, and Paloma Creek came tumbling out of the rocky cañon with an unceasing murmur. There was only one wagon and a drooping team before the low log building at the base of the rimrock.

Steve reined up some two hundred yards from Jack Black's place. "I'll come up easy while you have it out," he said.

"It won't take long."

Smoky galloped on. Walking his horse, Steve saw light shine out of the doorway as Smoky entered.

Moments later, off in the night, Steve heard a loping horse cutting across the range from the general direction of Lariat Cañon. A single rider. That would be Denver Red. Steve walked his horse to cut off the rider. The man was close before he pulled up sharply. A gun leaped into his hand.

"That you, Denver Red?"

"Who is it?"

"I'm with Smoky."

"It's you, is it?" said Denver Red unpleasantly. He holstered the gun and rode up. "Where's Smoky?"

"Talking to Jack Black. We'll wait here till they're done."

"Who says we will?"

"You heard me."

"Why, damn you!" exploded Denver Red, streaking for his gun.

Steve outdrew him. The moonlight glinted on his gun as he rapped: "Hold it!"

Denver Red's arms shot up. He swore under his breath. "What's comin' off here?"

"You're comin' off, mister. Keep 'em up, while I get your guns, and then climb down."

Denver Red uttered another oath as he dismounted, and his horse bolted away from Steve's slap.

"I don't like you," said Steve, "so take it easy ahead of me with your hands high. Smoky can handle you when he comes out. I've got business with Jack Black."

"What kinda business?" asked Denver Red sullenly.

"The kind that ought to have been done long ago. I'm bringing the wages of sin. Don't walk so fast. We've got plenty of time."

Denver Red's horse was making for the corrals behind the log building. Steve guessed the horse had been there before. Smoky was still inside. He wondered what Smoky was hearing.

Behind a fringe of mesquite brush across the road a horse nickered. Steve realized then his own horse already had pricked ears in that direction. He demanded: "Anybody else due to show up here with you?"

"Nobody," retorted Denver Red, staring at the spot. His hands came down slowly. "That ain't a stray horse!"

"Keep walking," ordered Steve.

A yell answered him, and it was not Denver Red.

"Cut 'em down, boys! This is good enough!"

A rifle cracked spitefully. That shot might have been the key that loosed the floodgates of hell. A roaring, rising crescendo of shots followed. A bullet knocked Steve back in the saddle. He felt a second slug tear through his Stetson crown, just above the scalp. For a second time that night a horse staggered under him in a weaving, helpless lurch that told its own story. It all happened instantaneously. Steve was thinking, acting in split seconds while it was happening.

Denver Red was plunging toward Jack Black's building in a dodging run that made him an uncertain target in the moonlight. Steve twisted down and out of the saddle while his horse still staggered. Once more he took the rifle, dropping Denver Red's guns. The horse screened him for a breath, and, as its legs buckled and bullets thudded into its body, Steve raced after Denver Red.

The chance was slim. They were gunning at him like a running rabbit. Unless his ears were mistaken that man who had opened fire with a shout was Buster Davis, venomous for a kill. There'd be no mercy. At least part of Caleb Reeves's posse had known where to come.

The night was full of crashing, screaming death. Dust spurted from the road in front of Steve's feet. He heard slugs screaming close. He lost his hat; it felt as if a bullet had knocked it off. A searing lash slapped across the back of his shoulder, and he knew that only his speed had carried him inches ahead of death.

Light gleamed as the door swung open. Smoky's short,

compact figure rushed out, behind him the hulking, bearded Jack Black. Back by the road, mesquite was crackling as riders galloped after the two fleeing men, emptying their guns as they came. Denver Red staggered, kept on with a limp. Jack Black plunged back inside. But Smoky stood there. Red streaks licked from his gun.

The wagon team was backing away from the hitch rack. Smoky's horse screamed as a bullet struck it, plunged back, tore the reins free, and bolted away.

Denver Red staggered through the lighted doorway as Steve raced up, calling: "Get inside, Smoky!"

Smoky dodged in and slammed the door. A wooden bar was leaning behind the door. Smoky slammed it down into place as Steve knocked the chimney from one of the lamps, extinguished the flame, and made for the other lamp. As the room plunged into darkness, Jack Black yelled in the kitchen.

"They're out by the corral! We're cornered in here!"

Denver Red was groaning and cursing. "You two brought 'em here, damn you!"

Somewhere in back, a woman began to wail in Spanish. The girl, Josita, faltered in the darkness: "*Señor* Smoky, will they keel us?"

"Get down on the floor behind the bar and stay there," Steve panted at her.

Glass crashed as a bullet bored into the room. Another bullet tore through the plank door. A rifle barked in the kitchen. Jack Black swore aloud with a savageness new to him. "Got one, by hell!"

Steve broke out a windowpane with his rifle muzzle and peered cautiously out. Smoky did the same at another window. The horsemen stopped, retreated to cover. Out there in the night, men were closing in on foot. Hugging the ground, they were hard to see.

171

"Ain't this one hell of a mess?" asked Smoky.

"They might have dropped us out there in the road!"

"They've got us!"

"Looks like it," agreed Steve. "I'm bleeding. My horse is down, and yours is gone. Any more around?"

"Some back in the corrals, I think."

"They ain't doin' us any good now." Steve turned his head. "What'd you find out, Smoky? Did he tell you?"

"He said my old man was a preacher over in East Texas," said Smoky in a tight voice. "Wouldn't it have to work out that way? My old man a sky pilot!"

A gun flashed out there in the night. Steve threw a bullet at the spot, didn't know whether he hit the man. The firing had slacked off. The posse was saving ammunition. In the kitchen, Jack Black was pouring shot after shot from the windows. Steve could hear him shifting about, hear his oaths and orders to Denver Red. "Damn your leg, Red! Stand up an' fight! I got enough cartridges to keep us goin' all night. Drive 'em away from the corrals! Damn them sheds! I should've torn 'em down a long time ago."

A shout came out of the night.

"Come out with your hands in the air! You'll get a fair trial in court!"

Steve answered. "There ain't any doubt what the trial'll be like!"

"That you, Cochrane?"

"That's me."

"You're a damned lyin' outlaw!" called Caleb Reeves from a depression nearby, where he was invisible. "But you was raised around here. You know I back up my word. You'll all get a fair trial. There'll be no vigilante mob stringing you up."

Smoky shouted: "Your sheriff's noose fits just as tight!

Come in an' get us!"

"We'll burn you out!" roared Caleb Reeves. "An' gun you when you come runnin' out from the fire. This is your last chance!"

"There's women in here!" Steve called.

"Send 'em out! They'll be safe enough!"

"Josita," Steve said, turning from the window. "Get your mother an' any other women an' walk out."

Only the two women were inside. They were both weeping as Steve unbarred the front door, let them slip quickly out, and barred the door again. Guns were silent while they ran to safety.

"Brother Jack," called Caleb Reeves, "you're tarred with the same stick. I've had my ideas about you for some time. That bunch that held up the Stag Bar in town was seen in your place earlier tonight, talkin' with you. Are you fightin' it out with 'em, or will you take a chance with the law?"

"I'll talk it over with you, Reeves," Jack Black called out. "Walk up to the front of the building. I'll step out with my hands up. If there's any double-crossin', you can gut-shoot me an' even the score."

Advice from the posse was audible.

"Don't do it, Caleb! It's a damned trick!"

"You can't trust snakes like that, Caleb!"

Jack Black called: "Are you afraid of a man with his hands in the air?"

"There ain't an outlaw livin' I'm afraid of!" shouted Reeves. "If you're workin' a trick, the posse'll get you. I'm a-comin'. Step out in front with your hands in the air!"

Denver Red protested bitterly as Jack Black left the kitchen. "You won't have any luck talkin', Jack. Are you crazy?"

"Watch them back windows," Jack ordered. "I know what I'm doin'."

"What *are* you doing?" Steve demanded as the big bearded man unbarred the front door.

Jack Black chuckled. It sounded malevolent with sinister humor. "I'm fixin' to get us outta here, fellow. Hold your horses. This ain't the night we hang, or I miss my guess. I always keep out an ace or two in a tight game."

Gunpowder fumes bit at the nostrils; the sudden quiet was almost as sinister as Jack Black's chuckle. The moonlight, flooding down on the dusty road, picked out with eerie clarity the two figures that moved into the open. Jack Black, huge, stoop-shouldered, bearded, hands high by his bald head, and the tall, spare, wary figure of the sheriff, who walked grimly, slowly, through the gloom, gun out, ready. They met near the hitch rack. Each word came clearly through the broken windows.

"What are you tryin' to do?" Caleb Reeves demanded.

Jack Black chuckled. "Talk easy, Sheriff. You got a surprise comin'. Maybe the posse better not know."

"Damn you, what kinda bluff are you runnin'?"

"I've heard about you, Reeves. You wasn't always a sheriff. One of them boys inside left East Texas when he was about five years old, an' never knew who his folks were. Are you willin' to burn him out an' shoot him up?"

"*Oh!*" Smoky gulped.

Steve hardly heard. He forgot for the moment he was holding a rifle. He was looking out into the moonlight, where Caleb Reeves stood, stiff and motionless. It was not possible that one man's voice could hold hope and agony, joy and grief, such as burst from Caleb Reeves. "My boy, my Jimmy's . . . in there?"

Smoky's agonized husk came: "Steve, Steve. I remember

now. She used to call me Jimmy."

Jack Black said: "Dirk Johnson told me the boy's mother married the wrong man, so he evened the score by takin' the kid and makin' an outlaw outta him. Your own flesh and blood, Reeves, your own son's in there. Are you a sheriff, or a father?"

There was not light enough to see tears, but Caleb Reeves's voice was strangled. "After all these years, I've got to see him. Jimmy, it's your dad comin' in." Caleb Reeves holstered his gun and walked into the dark room. "Jimmy, my son. . . ."

Voices from the posse were shouting.

"Caleb, what're you doin' in there?"

"You, Jack, stay out there where we can see you!"

Inside Smoky's voice was husky. "I've been lookin' . . . I never figured it'd be like this . . . trouble like this when I found you. My . . . my mother?"

Caleb Reeves cleared his throat. "Three years after you was taken from us, Son."

"I was ready to hear it," said Smoky. "And now, there's no use dodging it. I'm the man who held up the stage a couple of years ago, an' made that play tonight. You're the sheriff. I ain't expectin' anything."

Steve spoke. "He's been tryin' for years to find who his folks were. Jack Black, out there, promised to tell him if he'd clean out that safe tonight. He did it, and Black told him his father was a preacher in East Texas. That's all he knew till you walked up."

Caleb Reeves stood rigidly in the darkness and woodenly repeated: "I'm the sheriff."

"You heard me," said Smoky. "I'm not askin' for anything. I've got this comin', I guess."

"When it was plain we'd never get you back," said Caleb

175

Reeves, "I put down my Bible an' took up a gun. My hand has been against all outlaws since then." And out of the past, Caleb Reeves, the man of God, spoke the bitter truth he had once preached. " 'Those that live by the sword, shall die by the sword.' Oh, Lord, this is too heavy a burden to lay on me."

"The Bible," said Smoky, "ain't never been much to me. But I'll play my own game out. You're the sheriff. You can't quit it now when I've put you in a corner."

"I put my hand on the Bible," said Caleb Reeves, "an' took the oath to carry out the duties. I've shown no favors to any man's son. I can't do it now to mine."

"I'm tryin' to tell you," said Smoky gruffly.

Caleb Reeves gulped harshly. "Light a match, Son. Lemme look at your face."

Two matches sparked, flared.

Steve saw them in the glaring little circle of yellow light, father and son, two pale, strained faces staring hungrily at each other. The matches flickered out. The faces vanished.

"You're like your mother," said Caleb Reeves in a low voice. "Good bye, Son. . . ."

Caleb Reeves stumbled against the side of the door as he went out, walking like a blind man.

There was a jeering note of assurance in Jack Black's greeting. "Well, Sheriff, do we ride away from here?"

Caleb Reeves stared at him. "You knew this, an' never told me anything about it."

"Do you think I'd be fool enough to do that? I didn't know where he was. You'd 'a' been smokin' after me with a gun. Are you gonna fix it, Reeves?"

Caleb Reeves straightened. He seemed to tower in the moonlight. The threat in his voice had a scornful, warning edge. "Stand there till I get to cover. You'll get your answer quick."

VII
"THE DEATH CIRCLE"

Jack Black was swearing in his beard when the moment came for him to jump back inside. "What'd he say? What's he gonna do?"

"Kill you!" said Steve. "If we weren't in a tight all here together, I'd do it myself."

"You mean he'll gun his own flesh?"

A shout out in the night gave the answer. "Close in on 'em, boys!"

Jack Black rushed to the back windows as guns began to bark and roar.

Smoky said: "Steve, how can I throw down on them now? I might hit *him*."

"You made your choice. He wouldn't want you to go out like a rabbit."

Smoky's reply was cool. "I reckon so. Here goes hell."

Bullets were smashing through the plank door, screaming through the windows; bottles crashed behind the bar; the raw smell of whisky spread through the low-ceilinged room. The posse had spread out in a thin circle, was firing from all sides. Now and then a dark flit of movement showed in the moonlight as a posseman ducked forward to a closer bit of cover. They were moving in, tightening the death circle.

The log building had other rooms. Steve and Smoky moved from window to window, in and out of the rooms, watching all sides. Blood soaked Steve's back. Pain was grinding through his shoulder, but there was no time to waste on such matters. Jack Black passed out fresh boxes of ammunition. Their guns grew hot. Steve ducked behind the bar, knocked off the top of a bottle of beer, and slaked a burning thirst. He carried a bottle to Smoky at one of the front windows.

"Thanks," said Smoky. "Steve, the moon'll be up for hours yet. They must have sent back to town for more men."

"They'll have a hundred men out there in an hour or so," Steve agreed. "Every man in Costerville that can pack a gun will come fast."

"I'm thinking about him," muttered Smoky.

"Think about yourself."

"Hell, I'm a goner already. We all are. I'll say it again, Steve. I'm sorry you got drawn into this."

"Now you're talking like a fool. Look out the window there."

Smoky dropped the beer bottle, whipped his rifle to the window. "What is it?"

"I meant look up. See them clouds drifting in. I've been watching them."

"Pretty, ain't they?" said Smoky ironically. "Cloud gazing won't help you."

"Maybe it will," said Steve. "Those clouds are spotty, but they're drifting steady. They'll be over us in a little while. Maybe one of them'll cover the moon for a few minutes."

"You're grabbing at straws, Steve. Our hosses are gone. If Jack Black's got anything back in the corral, we ain't got a chance to catch it an' get goin'."

"The posse," said Steve calmly, "has got horses over there by the mesquite. The men are scattered out pretty thin right now. If we can get some shadow and run for it, we might have a chance of reaching their horses."

"Uhn-huh," said Smoky. After a moment he added: "It

178

might work, if a cloud gets over the moon an' more men from town aren't here yet, an' if we can buck through 'em an' get to the hosses. About one chance in a thousand, Steve."

"More'n we'll have if we stay here."

"Tell Jack Black about it."

"You're crazy!" was Jack Black's decision in the pitch-hued blackness of the kitchen. "Watch where you're steppin'. Red stood in front of the window too long an' got one in the face."

The posse was edging closer. Around the thin, imprisoning circle guns kept up a ceaseless, intermittent fire. It seemed that the clouds had stopped in the sky, that time was rushing past with frantic haste, while more possemen from Costerville were coming fast. But gradually the first scattered clouds drifted overhead, and behind them crawled other patches of heavier clouds.

"It's coming," said Steve. "Fill your gun belt, Smoky."

"I'm ready!" said Smoky tersely.

The white, bright moonlight began to dim, fade away. Shadows grew deeper, blacker outside.

"All right, Smoky," Steve clipped out, and went into the kitchen. "Coming with us?" he asked Jack Black.

"Hell, yes, I reckon so."

Gun muzzles were flickering red and clear in the new darkness outside. The corrals were almost invisible now as the high, dark cloud overhead blotted out the moon.

"To the left, toward the mesquite," said Steve. "Every man for himself."

Steve jerked open the door and dived out, rifle in his left hand, cocked six-gun in his right, and they were instantly three racing shadows.

For a moment or two the possemen did not realize what was happening. Then a yell of warning rang out. A gun streaked red. Steve poured a shot at the spot. Another gun a few yards off to the left opened up. Steve fired that way. Over to the right, Jack Black's six-gun was roaring. But between them, Smoky's gun was silent. Smoky was running without shooting—only a man who had heard that meeting between father and son would understand why.

A gun blasted at Smoky's vague, rushing figure. Steve saw the vicious, red muzzle spurt, and turned his gun that way, blasting his last two shots. The man gave ground, dodging away, and that would not be Caleb Reeves who ran.

Then suddenly they were even with the wide-spaced possemen, then past them, dashing toward the looming mesquite before the nearest possemen realized their purpose. But quickly shots rained after them. Warning shouts bawled raucously through the night.

The clouds began to drift on past the moon. Light swiftly seeped back as they plunged into the fringe of the mesquite. Sharp thorns tore at them. Just ahead, horses were stamping, snorting. A man was swearing angrily. The gunfire died away as the possemen realized their horses were in danger of being shot.

Smoky was not fast. Steve slowed to keep near him. Jack Black, for all his age, was ahead of them when the man who was watching the horses challenged them. Jack Black's gun opened up, shot after shot, and the man dropped. Jack Black was winging up on one of the plunging, rearing horses as Smoky and Steve ran up. He was pulling away when the man he had shot down staggered up to a knee and emptied a handgun at him. Jack Black grabbed the saddle horn, hung for a second, and fell heavily under the hoofs of stampeding horses.

Steve had grabbed two horses. He shoved reins into Smoky's hand. Smoky dragged himself into the saddle. They rode off with the bolting horses.

From behind them shouts of rage, the crackle of gunfire, increased, and then fell swiftly back as the furiously ridden horses thundered across a shallow arroyo, through another belt of mesquite, and on into the open night. Another cloud drew over the moon, and over his shoulder Steve saw more and more clouds drifting up. There would be no clear moonlight the rest of the night. Riding close, he and Smoky raced into the west, into the Jawbone Mountain country, and there were few horses left for the posse to follow them quickly.

When they stopped the lathered horses miles beyond for a few moments' rest, there was no sound of pursuit. The clouds were thicker now. Tracks would be almost impossible to follow until daybreak.

"There's a rope on this saddle," said Steve. "Remember those horses over by Jawbone Mountain? We can saddle fresh by daybreak, and outride any trackers before night. South of the border, you can let the old man know you're safe, and where he can meet you if he wants to visit."

"Sounds good," muttered Smoky. "Let's get goin'."

They pushed the horses, hour after hour, across the lowlands, across the piñon ridges and the grass country beyond. The moon went down, and, after a short period of blackness, the gray false dawn began to creep in from the east. The foothill slopes of Jawbone Mountain were just ahead.

They were climbing the slopes of Jawbone Mountain when the crimson dawn broke behind them. They topped a ridge and saw in the mountain valley beyond a small bunch of grazing horses.

"There we are," said Steve. "I'll get a couple."

Smoky had not spoken for an hour. He was clutching the saddle horn now. His face was gray and lined. He turned and looked back over the wide valley into the crimson dawn, and his voice was strained. "I'm stoppin' here, Steve."

Then Steve saw that Smoky's hand was red with dried blood, and blood had oozed down the saddle and flying drops spotted the white patches of the wary pinto pony.

"Why'n hell didn't you tell me you were wounded?" Steve rapped out as he dismounted hastily and stepped to Smoky.

Smoky tried to dismount and fell into Steve's arms, and Steve lowered him gently. Smoky lay on the ground, panting. He tried to lift his head. Steve rolled his coat quickly and put it under Smoky's head.

"I got it while we was runnin' for the hosses," Smoky muttered. "I figured you'd try to stay with me if I didn't keep ridin'."

"I'll get you to a house somewhere, an' have 'em send for a doctor."

"An' have the Costerville men comin' for me?" said Smoky. A faint smile came over his face. He shook his head. "No danger of that, Steve. I can feel it comin'. Roll me a quirly."

With shaking fingers, Steve rolled a cigarette, put it between Smoky's lips, and held a match.

"I reckon we're safe enough here for a little," said Smoky. "They won't be tracking us good till daylight. It'll be hours before they get this far."

"I can ride back and cut them off, throw them off the trail."

Smoky ignored that. They both knew it was only talk. "He'll be leadin' 'em," Smoky muttered. "He'll find me. Write him a letter when you can, Steve, an' tell him the things I didn't get a chance to say. You'll do that?"

"Anything you ask, pardner."

Smoky finished the cigarette. His face was white. He was

taking shallow, quick breaths.

Great streamers of color led the glowing rim of the rising sun above the far horizon. Smoky lifted his head and stared at the beauty of the sunrise for a moment, and then dropped back heavily. Once more a faint smile came on his face. His eyes were staring up at the thinning clouds and bright blue sky as he spoke, and it seemed to Steve that Smoky was talking to something up there in the sky, something that only Smoky could see. " 'Those that live by the sword shall die by the sword.' I reckon, if it's good enough for him, it's good enough for me," Smoky muttered. "This oughta help even things up."

Smoky was still smiling faintly up at the sky when Steve suddenly realized that he was alone, and turned blindly away. When he turned back, Smoky's eyes were closed, and Smoky seemed to be peacefully resting.

Steve rode down the slope, roped a fresh horse, and shifted his saddle.

Hours later he was waiting beside Smoky when the first dust of riders on their trail showed miles away. Steve swung on his horse then. It would not be long until the possemen reached this spot. He paused, looking down for the final time at Smoky before he started the long, hard ride toward the border.

"He'll find you, Smoky," Steve said aloud. "And my guess is, he'll be proud of you, like I'm proud of you. Like . . ." —Steve looked up at the blue sky where Smoky had last looked—"like I reckon she's proud of you for not comin' out last night with your gun smokin'. I reckon everything is all right now. So long, pardner."

Steve headed into the south from there, and he was smiling. Smoky would want it that way. Smiling. For Smoky was going home, one prodigal whose folks would understand and be proud.

PRODIGAL OF DEATH

The fifth story T. T. Flynn wrote in 1936 was completed in March. His agent sent it to Rogers Terrill at Popular Publications who bought it at once for *Dime Western*. In the event, it was published instead in *Star Western* (11/36) under the title "A Prodigal for Boothill." By the author's count, it was 12,000 words. He was paid $240.00 for it upon acceptance. Flynn's title for the story was "Hell for the Prodigal." That title has been modified for its appearance in this collection. Having been somewhat wild in his own youth and always very much one who defied the herd, Ted Flynn knew in a deeply personal way the feelings of being an outsider, of being self-sufficient and yet desperate, and it was from the depths of early sorrow that he could evoke, as few others have been able so intimately, the isolation and awkwardness of the loner when he returns and finds that the past has managed to seal itself away forever. Vengeance was rarely a theme for T. T. Flynn in his stories, but rather, when possible, acceptance and reconciliation.

I

"THE WAGON SPOKE"

Dike Kennedy eased silently away from the winking little campfire and watched his horse's ears. The sable night sky cupped a three-quarter moon over the sparsely wooded slopes of the San Gabriel Pass. Piñon pine and smaller growth hid the rutted road below the long, easy slope. The cool, sweet breeze of late evening brought the weird yapping of distant coyotes. But the gray gelding's ears were not pointed back through the pass toward the coyote clamor. Something down the slope toward the road held the gelding's attention.

Dike Kennedy loosened his gun in the holster and faded out of the little clearing where the fire glowed comfortably near his bedroll.

The coyotes fell silent. An owl hooted. The breeze sighed through the treetops—and down the slope a stick cracked. Something scraped against a stone. It sounded like a boot sole. Drawing his gun, Dike Kennedy moved silently to meet the intruder.

Soft, scuffling feet became audible. A panting voice uttered a low oath.

"Goin' somewhere, stranger?" Dike asked curtly.

The black figure of a man stopped with a startled oath. His reply was hasty. "It's all right. I ain't sneakin' up on anybody. I'm lookin' for Dike Kennedy. I heard he was stoppin' here in the pass tonight."

"I'm Kennedy. Why in hell didn't you yell?"

"I saw the campfire, but I didn't aim to advertise my business to strangers. I'm Felix Morton. I guess you remember me."

"Uhn-huh . . . but it ain't to your credit," Dike said curtly. "If you're alone, walk on to the fire."

Breathing hard, Felix Morton stopped by the fire and passed a bandanna over his face. He was a stoutish man, wearing black trousers tucked into riding boots and a black, low-crowned hat set squarely on his head. He removed the hat, and a bald spot showed. Morton's eyes were wide-set and crafty under arched, bushy brows.

"That Mex, Pablo Sanchez, who passed you this afternoon said you aimed to stop here in the pass tonight," Morton said. "It struck me we might do some business. I reckon, Kennedy, there's only one reason brings you back to Wagon Spoke range."

Dike was rolling a cigarette. "What d'you figure it was?" he questioned casually.

Felix Morton hesitated. "Trane Lamar," he said finally, and peered through the fire glow to see the effect.

Nothing was visible on Kennedy's face. "What made you figger I had any interest in Trane Lamar?"

Felix Morton passed the bandanna over his face again and spread his hands behind to the warmth of the fire. The older man eyed Kennedy and made bold to sneer slightly. "If you didn't come back with Trane Lamar on your mind, you should have. I reckon word's reached you, wherever you've been these six, seven years, that Trane Lamar was behind the killin' of your brother Bud. Trane's got the Wagon Spoke brand now an' all the land your father left. It was plain to everyone that Lamar crowded Bud one way an' another until he got Bud outta the way an' scooped in the Wagon Spoke land."

"I've heard all that," Dike admitted slowly.

"That's what brought me out here to see you," Morton confided. "I figgered you'd come back gunnin' for Trane Lamar. That's why I came, Dike. My partner, Sim Beasley, an' myself are after Lamar's scalp, too. He's had things his own way too long on the Wagon Spoke range. Sim an' I have been waitin' for years to take him down a peg."

"Sounds like you and Sim Beasley," Kennedy remarked laconically. "You always was a couple of tight lawyers, wasn't you?"

Morton chuckled his gratification. "We know the law anyway, an' a few tricks besides. Now here's the point. We've had a drought two years runnin'. Beef prices have dropped. Trane Lamar was so greedy for land he grabbed off too much. Trane is caught short, an' he borrowed his credit out around here. Sim an' I figgered we had him three months ago. But we didn't, because he pulled some of that Lamar luck," Morton said sourly. "Some people he knew back East lent him a tidy pile of money on his personal note. So it looks like he'll ride through, barrin' nothin' else happens."

"Did you ride fifteen miles out here to tell me that?"

Morton hesitated and shrugged. "I rode out here to make a deal with you, Kennedy. One that'll put you on your feet, ownin' the Wagon Spoke again, with cash in the bank, an' at the same time wind up everything right an' handy for Sim an' me."

"I'm listenin'."

Morton coughed. "If Trane Lamar was outta the way, that Eastern money'd be called back. That'd cut the bottom out from under the Lamar holdings. They'd fall apart like a tumbleweed stack in a norther."

"Lamar's got a daughter?"

"You oughta know. You kep' company with her when

she was a kid, didn't you?"

"Never mind that."

"Nothin' personal," Morton denied hastily. "But Carole Lamar'll never be able to keep what her old man got together, once it starts to fall apart. I've got that fixed up already. All we need is Lamar outta the way."

"Seems to me you'd have done it before this."

Morton coughed again. He looked uncomfortable. "Lamar's a bad man with a gun. Most of his men'd follow him through hell. Sim an' I ain't found anyone we can *trust* to do the job. But when I heard you'd come back an' was sorta lookin' the land over before you showed up, I knew you was the man, Dike."

Dike flicked his cigarette into the fire. Sparks floated up and showed his face impassive. "I reckon you feel you can trust me, huh?" he said mildly.

"Shore. Ain't our eggs all in the same box? Didn't Lamar bust you an' Carole up years ago? 'Scuse me . . . that slipped out. But this is a business now. An' I guess we can do business, eh?" Morton chuckled, rubbing his hands.

"Maybe I'm kinda dumb," Dike said slowly. "But what's this business you're countin' on me to do?"

Morton chuckled again, as if they enjoyed a joke together. "Just get Lamar outta the way, Dike."

"I thought I heard you say that, but I wanted to make sure." Dike sighed. "If I kill Trane Lamar, I get title to the Wagon Spoke, an' cash money besides?"

"That's right," Morton assented eagerly.

"Suppose I get caught?" he asked.

"Sim an' I'll get you off. We know the law. Folks don't feel any too good toward Lamar. They know about Bud. We can pick a jury that'd shake your hand as you walked out free."

"Uhn-huh . . . I'll bet you could. Any objection to me

shootin' Lamar in the back?"

"Suit yourself, Dike. It'd probably be safer." Morton grinned.

Dike grinned broadly, also, but there was no mirth on his face. His fist lashed out and knocked the cow-town lawyer back into the campfire.

Morton scrambled up, showering sparks and crying in choked surprise and fear: "My god, Kennedy, I thought we was f-friends! D-don't do it!"

"Makes me mad just to think you had an idea I'd listen to your yapping. I'm gonna purify your mind, Morton."

Dike hit him again.

II

"ENEMY'S RANGE"

The coyotes were yapping in the distance as Dike tucked in the end of his pack rope and turned back to the dying fire where Felix Morton lay unconscious on the ground. The lawyer was not an old man. He was strong enough to take a beating and go down fighting wildly. Dike knelt and felt Morton's pulse. It was beating strongly. Morton was already beginning to breathe heavily and mutter. He'd be on his feet shortly.

"There's some laws that ain't in your books," Dike growled, rising to his feet. "You'd better have 'em down pat when we meet again."

He swung into the saddle and rode down the slope, leading the pack horse. The urge to sleep was gone. Anyway, he'd be a fool to try it after Morton left. If he read the man right, his own life wasn't any too safe now.

Out of the San Gabriel Pass, Dike rode down toward the lonely sweep of the Wagon Spoke range spreading out below under the silver moon wash. A lump came into his throat, and a hardness that had remained in him for years softened and vanished. This was his home range. Here he had spent years as a kid. Here lay memories he never could recapture. Every arroyo and hill, every little stream and cottonwood and rutted road was familiar and friendly.

True, there'd be no mother at the old ranch house with, perhaps, a fresh-filled cookie jar, but she was here, everywhere, on this sleeping range below the San Gabriel Pass. The old man was gone, and Bud was gone. Yet Trane Lamar could not kill or foreclose on the past. Dike had meant to ride down out of the pass with the rising sun, seeing again the country as it had been that early morning years before when he had ridden out through the pass for good. Now, Felix Morton had spoiled that plan.

So Dike Kennedy came home in the moonlight, and turned off across the open range. An hour or so after midnight he made camp again under a towering cottonwood beside a shallow arroyo.

The hot, rising sun brought him out of the blankets. With the last water from his canteens he made coffee. Presently he was riding again across land he knew well—the rolling, open land of Trane Lamar's home ranch, the Circle Z.

Felix Morton had been right. Drought lay heavily on this western side of the mountains. The few cattle in sight were gaunt and poor. Teapot Creek, that always had held water, was dry.

Dike cut over toward a windmill that was barely turning in the light wind. A thin trickle of water dripped into the half-empty, galvanized tank. The dirt tank to one side, for the overflow, was a circle of sun-cracked mud, except for one damp, hoof-churned spot at the end. Half a hundred bony steers waited around the stout wire that fenced in the windmill and bawled for the water they could not reach.

Opening the gate, Dike led his horse in and carefully watered it. He drank himself, and filled his canteens, and then took time to wash and shave, for no good reason.

"You're a damned fool, Dike," he informed his reflection in the water. Then he carefully combed his hair and felt more sheepish than ever. Nevertheless he was a lanky, handsome figure as he rode on, his black Stetson tip-tilted slightly on his head.

He was twenty-six—seven years older than the nineteen-year-old wild, reckless youngster who had ridden off the Wagon Spoke range for good, leaving everything to twenty-four-year old Bud. He remembered Bud's last words now.

"You worried hell outta Maw before she died, Dike," his brother had said. "You gave the old man plenty of bad nights wonderin' what next you'd be up to. We've got to scratch an' dig between us. If you ain't willin' to scratch, light out on your own. I ain't got time to be bothered."

Then, that same night, Trane Lamar had come to his door instead of Carole and snapped: "If I ketch you around here lookin' for Carole again, I'll have you tied to a wagon gate an' whipped offa my land! You're a no-account tramp, an' you ain't wanted around here!"

Dike had almost gone for his gun, but instead he had ridden off in a blind fury that had turned into a resentful, stubborn anger. That dawn had found him riding out for good.

Now, seven years had hardened, steadied, yet not entirely wiped out the dancing devils of recklessness and humor in

191

Dike's gray eyes. At times, in profile, he looked hard, grim.

Toward noon he skirted the small hill that broke the north winds from the Circle Z ranch buildings. A new corral had been built and a couple more outbuildings had been put up. Several rooms had been added to the huge adobe house. But it was the same. It was Trane Lamar's home and bigger and better than any other on the Wagon Spoke range, just as Trane Lamar counted himself bigger and better than any other man in the county.

His heart began to thump as he rode toward the house and saw a slender figure in a sunbonnet cutting flowers before the long front verandah. She hadn't changed much. Yes, she had. She was a woman now, slender and assured as she watched him ride up. Then puzzled, unbelieving, she called: *"Dike?"*

What did you say after seven years? Dike was wordless as he swung down. Carole's cry had been startled surprise; now she stood, holding an armful of flowers with a look on her small, oval face he couldn't fathom. "Seems like I've been gone a mighty long time," Dike found himself saying coolly.

Carole smiled uncertainly. "You've changed, Dike. Are . . . are you going to stay long?"

"Depends."

Hell—he might be in a tight poker game for all the feeling he was getting into his face and words! What he felt, what he *wanted* to say, wouldn't come through the grim mask he'd come to adopt in a tight corner.

She wasn't asking him to sit down. It was about time to eat. He could smell food cooking inside. She wasn't saying anything about a meal. She said: "How long have you been back, Dike?"

"Just came."

"I'm . . . I'm glad you dropped by here."

But she didn't sound as if she were glad. She looked

uneasily toward the front door. Dike knew the truth then. He'd been gone so long it seemed as if the past had faded into mere memory, but here they hadn't forgotten. Dike told her in a way he'd never meant to, curtly, gruffly: "I stopped by to see your father on some business."

"Oh!" Funny how much meaning Carole packed in that one little word! "I . . . I don't think he feels very well today, Dike. Could you see him some other time? He's going into town tomorrow."

Carole sounded as if she were pleading. Her face was red. Dike was smiling with cold unbelief when the front door opened and Trane Lamar stepped out on the verandah, as huge, erect, and healthy as he'd ever been.

III

"WHIPS FOR A PRODIGAL"

The only change in Trane Lamar was the iron gray in his hair and mustache. Otherwise, he was the same tall, powerful man with the cold eyes, a stern mouth, and a brusque manner. As was his habit, Lamar came to the point at once. "One of the men brought word from town last night you were headin' back into these parts, Kennedy. I was wondering if you'd have the nerve to come on Circle Z land again. If you've forgotten what I told you the last time you were here, I'll say it again. Carole, you'd better go in the house."

"I'd rather not," Carole refused. "Dike tells me he came to see you."

"I've got no business with him!"

Dike grinned bleakly. He was on firm ground again. He

hadn't been sure whether he'd say it. Carole could have changed him. She hadn't. "Maybe you'd better go in, Carole," Dike suggested in a voice even colder than he meant it to be. "I aim to do some plain talkin'."

"I think I'd rather hear it." Carole was pale now.

"Suit yourself." Dike addressed Trane Lamar. "About a month ago I heard that Bud'd been murdered two years back, an' you'd foreclosed on our ranch an' bought it at a sheriff's sale. I've come back to look into that deal, Lamar."

"You'll find it on the county books at the courthouse."

"Will I find a record of who murdered Bud?"

"They never got the man."

"Never proved it on him, you mean."

Trane Lamar had stepped off the verandah. He was scowling. They were not more than half a dozen paces apart now. Between them had fallen the icy wariness of men aware that a false word or move might end in flaming guns. Lamar spoke with suppressed fury. "Damn you! What do you mean by that?"

"Got you worried, hasn't it, Lamar?" Dike taunted bitterly.

"I'll take that outta your skin!" Lamar bawled, going for his gun.

Carole was moving before her father finished speaking. Her cry of protest was blotted out by the roar of Dike's gun. Dirt whipped from the ground just beyond Carole as the bullet struck there.

Dike dropped the gun as he cried out. For he had almost killed her, so instantaneously, so automatically had his hand moved in that flashing draw. All his attention had been on Trane Lamar. He hadn't suspected Carole's move until she had come between them; then the hammer had already been falling; only a split second had remained to turn the gun muzzle aside. By the grace of God he'd done it.

Now he stood, white-faced and shaking at the thought of the heavy lead slug tearing into Carole's slim body.

Trane Lamar swept his daughter aside with a long, powerful arm, ignoring her demands that he put up his gun. The big man was pale, also. Trane Lamar, who always had been proud of his speed with a gun, had been outdrawn by another man. If his daughter had not flashed in front of him, he would have been shot down before his gun was out.

Carole might not have known that, but Dike did. And Trane Lamar did, too. The knowledge seemed to fan Lamar's black fury. His voice rasped: "Keep outta this, Carole! Put your hands up, Kennedy, or, by God, I'll kill you as you stand!"

Dike lifted his hands. Lamar meant the threat. Four of Lamar's men came running around the corner of the house.

"Tie this man with his shirt off to the tailgate of a wagon an' hitch a team on!" Lamar grated.

"What are you going to do?" Carole demanded wildly.

"I told you to get into the house, Carole!"

"I won't! You two can't fight like this! Nothing's been said to cause it! Dike, I . . . I hate you for even thinking Bud was killed by anyone from the Circle Z! And Dad, if you . . . you don't come to your senses, I'll h-hate you, too!"

But her anger and fright were lost on her father. As the men caught Dike's arms, Trane Lamar swung his daughter around before him and marched her into the house.

Dike submitted. The men had guns. They were four, and two more came to meet them and help. Only one of the men was familiar—Bart Clagg, stocky, bowlegged, and surly, who never had liked Kennedy in the past and seemed no different now.

Dike was tied to the tailgate of the wagon, feet on the

ground, arms spread-eagled out to the sides of the wagon, and bound securely. The team was hitched into place when Trane Lamar strode out to them.

Lamar's face was black, forbidding; his manner had all the unheeding arrogance that had driven him through the years. "Kennedy, seven years ago I warned you if ever I caught you here again, I'd have you tied to a wagon an' whipped off my land. I'm keepin' my word. Jack, climb on that seat an' start him walkin'. Tom, take that whip an' lay it on all the way to the south gate."

The man called Tom was lean and sandy-haired; he spat brown tobacco juice on the ground, and hesitated. "Hell, Mister Lamar, I never whipped no man. It don't set right with me. . . ."

"All right, I won't order you to," Lamar said impatiently. "Clagg, how about you? Maybe your memory's as long as mine."

Clagg nodded. "I'll do it," he said briefly. "He should've had it long ago."

Dike spoke thickly: "You caught an advantage on this you didn't deserve, Lamar. If that whip hits me once at your orders, I'll never rest until it's squared between us!"

Lamar ignored him. He spoke to his men. "Sam, ride after us with horses. Jack, start drivin'. Clagg, let's see if your arm is strong enough to make a worthless wolf whine."

The south gate was two miles from the ranch house, two miles of futile anger, of shame and pain that cut deeper than ever Bart Clagg's whip could cut into skin and flesh. When the wagon stopped outside the south gate, Dike's back held raw welts and drying blood. He was feverish, dizzy, parched, weak. But his head was up. His eyes were fixed with a terrible intensity on Trane Lamar when the big man spoke curtly from the horse he had ridden the last mile.

"Untie him," Trane Lamar directed. When that was done, Lamar said icily: "There's your horses an' shirt, Kennedy. I'll send your gun into town this afternoon. You've been whipped like a dog. If you care to hang around these parts after this, stay outta my way."

Dike's answer was hoarse. "Are you intending to bring my gun to Palomar yourself, Lamar?"

"That'll be as it suits my pleasure," Lamar replied curtly. He reined back through the gate, saying: "Men, there's a heap of work to do yet this afternoon with that bunch of steers over in the Alameda draw."

Silently the men followed him, as if oppressed by the spectacle of a man whipped and shamed. Dike pulled his shirt on over his raw back, and rolled a cigarette with shaking hands, and drew great lungsful of smoke as he watched them out of sight.

His face was drawn and hard as the angles of a sandstone cliff when he climbed stiffly into the saddle and rode off across the range, on a roundabout way toward Palomar.

Silently he rode on beside Nestor Creek, where the cottonwoods grew tall and stately, and the dun-colored adobe houses grew out of the friendly earth. Low in the west the hot sun blazed crimson through dusty, lower air. Flour-like road dust jetted in little spurts each time a hoof struck the ground.

Memories waited here. There was the frame schoolhouse, still unpainted, weathered, with the little sagging cupola over the door. Farther on was the Red Dog Saloon—**High-Low Casey, Prop.**—where the card games had been high and wild, and there Ben Livermore's Ventana Bar, where Big May Castleman and her girls had danced away the pay of many a cowpoke on many a Saturday night. Next door was the narrow, shabby, three-roomed law office of Morton and Beasley, who knew a few tricks not in the law books.

Sim Beasley's hunched, wizened figure was standing before the door. He stared, then ducked into the office in the manner of a rabbit scuttling into his burrow.

Dike watched the office door as he rode past. If Felix Morton was up and about today, he might be fool enough to cut loose with a rifle from the shelter of the office. But Dike hardly thought so. The nature of the man was to do it some other way, some way covered by the law books.

Painfully Dike dismounted before Izzy's Emporium that stocked everything from a horse collar to a toothbrush. There, a busted cowpoke could always borrow ten dollars from the good-natured Izzy. But no more than that. Izzy had blind faith that ten dollars would buy any man a good drunk, and more would be wasted.

Izzy's store was doing a brisk business, with half a dozen people inside and two clerks busy. But Izzy, after one sharp look at the newcomer, deserted the customer he was serving and rushed out from behind the counter.

"You knocked my eye out, Dike! Didn't I know you quick as you come in? Where you been all these years? Golly, I'm glad to see you!"

Izzy was nodding and smiling and winking mysteriously as he wrung Dike's hand. "Come back in my office an' talk it over," he urged, and called over his shoulder: "I'll be with you in a minute, Miz Boatner."

Dike grinned. "Wait on the lady, Izzy. I'll walk over here an' pick me a gun outta your stock."

"A gun? You want a gun, Dike?" Izzy took in the empty holster. "Sure, you better have a gun. I'll get you one now, right away," he said hastily. "Just a minute, Miz Boatner. I'm comin' right now," Izzy promised as he hurried over to the gun case with Dike. Under his breath Izzy groaned: "You shouldn't ought to have come in town without no gun, Dike.

It positively ain't healthy."

"Ain't it, now?" Dike grinned, forgetting other matters in the cheer of seeing this old friend again. "Why the hell are you making faces at me, Izzy?"

For Izzy was staring past him toward the door. A stricken look came over Izzy's face. He snatched a new .45 and a box of cartridges out of the showcase and slid them across the glass. "Load it quick," Izzy whispered agonizingly. "There's Tom Trotter, the sheriff."

Behind Dike a cold voice warned: "Hands off that gun, Kennedy."

IV
"HANG-TREE BAIT"

Tom Trotter had been a rancher seven years past, and a good rancher. He was evidently a good sheriff now, for his gun was out as he advanced, and there was no hesitation or uncertainty in his manner. Men had evidently followed him to the store. They crowded through the doorway when they saw there was no danger of flying lead.

"You're under arrest, Kennedy," Tom Trotter said. "Put that gun back, Izzy. He won't need it."

Trotter was a big man, carelessly dressed, easy in his movements, but his curt order made Izzy hurriedly replace the gun.

"I reckon you know why I'm arrested," Dike said, waiting.

Trotter held out a hunting knife. "This is yours, ain't it, with DK burned in the handle?"

Narrow-eyed, Dike nodded slowly. "It's mine," he agreed.

"I must've lost it outta my pack. Where'd you find it?"

"By your campfire in San Gabriel Pass, where you cut Felix Morton's throat with it. You're under arrest for murder, Kennedy."

Behind Dike, Izzy sighed audibly. Izzy had known it was coming, had tried to warn, to help. Stunned, Dike eyed the half-circle of scowling men beyond the sheriff.

One of them growled: "Any man who'd cut a feller's throat like a hawg at killin' time oughta be strung up right off."

"By God, I'll have no talk like that!" Tom Trotter exclaimed violently. "This man's my prisoner now. Kennedy, why'd you kill him?"

Dike's wandering eye saw Sim Beasley, hovering on the flank of the group, rubbing his hands nervously together. He understood now why the wizened little lawyer had ducked out of sight so quickly. Chances were he'd gone out the back way for the sheriff.

"What makes you think *I* killed Morton?" Dike argued coolly. "Would I be damn' fool enough to leave a man there by my campfire where he'd be sure to be found?"

"You seem to have been a damn' fool, all right. Where'd you get that blood on your shirt?"

"It's off my back." Wooden-faced, Dike told them the truth, since Trane Lamar would spread it soon enough anyway.

Surprised exclamations, low oaths greeted that. Even Trotter was taken aback. Out of the corner of his eye Dike could see the women customers in a tense little knot listening.

Tom Trotter spoke harshly: "So Lamar had you whipped? You must be an all-around bad customer. What'd you do at the Circle Z?"

Not all the men wore guns. Trotter was the only one who
had a gun out. Even he seemed off his guard for a moment
from the amazing admission he had just heard.

"I was lookin' out for my interests . . . like I'm doin' now. I
don't see. . . ." Dike was still speaking as his left hand
knocked the gun off its aim. His fist traveled through the
blasting roar of the shot to a smashing impact on the sheriff's
jaw.

The bullet missed him by the span of a little finger. The
blow spun Trotter off balance. But Trotter held hard to the
gun as Dike wrenched at it. Instead of reeling back, Trotter
staggered forward, so that they both brought up hard against
the showcase.

The women were screaming, scattering to the back of the
store. Dike's fist caught the sheriff's jaw again. He had to get
Trotter's gun to have any chance of holding them off. As he
had planned, the sheriff's body screened him. He felt the gun
twisting out of Trotter's weakening grip.

All the black fury bred by Trane Lamar's whip flared in
Dike as he wrenched savagely at the weapon. Just as it came
free in his hands, his head seemed to explode from a blow at
the back.

Slipping into a hazy fog, collapsing down the front of the
showcase, Dike's last conscious thought was that Izzy had
slugged him. Izzy, too, had turned on him.

Doc Rumboldt closed his little black bag, adjusted his
steel-bowed spectacles to a more lop-sided position on his
nose

"That cut in your head'll heal up pretty quick, Dike," he
said cheerfully. "An' your back'll be as well as ever in a few
days." Doc put a pinch of snuff under his lip and carefully
closed the little round box. "You're lucky your skull wasn't

cracked open," he cheered. "Izzy never hit anyone with a gun barrel before. They say he swung it like he was choppin' through a piece of stove wood."

"Damn Izzy," Dike groaned. "What'd you do with my horses, Trotter?"

"They're at the livery stable," Tom Trotter said sourly as he slammed the cell door after Doc Rumboldt and turned the key.

The two men went out together. Dike sat on the edge of the cot and smoked a cigarette.

Seven years—and he'd come back to this! Chances were he was going to hang. Felix Morton had told Beasley where he was going. When Morton hadn't returned by morning, Beasley had told the sheriff, and Trotter had ridden out there and found Morton lying by the dead ashes of the campfire with his throat gashed open. The hunting knife was on the ground nearby. Felix Morton had told Dike he had come to the pass alone, and he couldn't have lain there by the fire more than a few minutes. Someone must have been close. Before Dike had reached the road, Morton's throat must have been cut. But why?

Dike rolled a cigarette. Who could have been there near the campfire? Had someone followed Morton from Palomar to kill the lawyer? If so, why had he waited? Fifteen miles was a long way to follow a man when the killing could have been done so easily any mile of the trip. Dike had dropped the knife in the fight with Morton or the hasty packing which had followed. The killer had picked it up, used it, and then left it there, knowing the owner would be blamed for the killing. But why?

Trotter's deputy brought him a tray of supper. The deputy was a long, rangy, young fellow with a big Adam's apple that bobbed up and down as he spoke.

"They're talkin' about hangin' you tonight," he informed Dike.

"They'll know where to find me," Dike said. "Is Trane Lamar in town?"

"Uhn-huh."

"Helpin' with the hangin' talk?"

"Can't tell you that."

"Were you Trotter's deputy when my brother Bud was shot?"

"Uhn-huh."

"Just what happened?"

"Never found out. Bud'd come into town on business. His horse turned up at the corral that night with an empty saddle. They found Bud next day, off the road a piece. He'd been plugged through the lung from behind."

"That's what I heard," Dike said grimly. "Wasn't there no tracks?"

"Sorta," the deputy said reluctantly. "I helped Tom Trotter foller 'em. We lost 'em finally up Teacup Creek. We never did find out where he come from."

"Over in Trane Lamar's patch of the range?"

"Anybody could've rode over thataway, I guess."

Dike flipped his cigarette out through the window bars. "Then Lamar foreclosed on Bud's place?"

"I've heard Lamar'd already served notice on Bud he was gonna foreclose. Bud'd got the promise of a loan from Felix Morton that day. Bud told it hisself before he left town. He was feelin' high over it." The deputy shook his head. "Bud even passed the remark, jokin' that Lamar'd have to kill him now to get the Wagon Spoke. There was hard feelin' against Lamar, but nobody ever could prove he had a hand in it."

"Did Felix Morton bid on the Wagon Spoke at the sheriff's sale?"

203

"Now you speak of it, he did. I recollect Morton put in a coupla low bids, an' stopped when Lamar topped 'em. Anything else you wanna know?"

"A hell of a lot," Dike growled. "But *you* don't know the answers."

V

"HIDE-AND-SEEK WITH DEATH"

Out in the street a gun roared in a roll of shots. A chorus of exuberant yells followed. Somebody was getting drunk. Through the open window Dike could see a bit of the street. More men than usual were moving about. Presently some men rode back along the side of the jail.

"You there, Kennedy?"

"Who's that?" Dike called through the window.

"Never mind, you pig-stickin' wolf! We're comin' to get you by 'n' by!"

They rode off whooping.

Sheriff Tom Trotter came to the cell door. He was grim. "I hate to think of gettin' shot by some crazy fool just to save your ornery skin, Kennedy. But I thought I'd tell you, if they rush the jail, I'll try to hold 'em off."

"You might gimme a gun an' let me help, Trotter."

"You got your hands on your last gun when you grabbed mine," Trotter said sourly as he walked out.

The hullabaloo outside the jail increased. Some men slipped around to the back. Shouts, angry voices, now and then a whoop and a gunshot came from the front.

Trotter's loud voice rang out in the night. "The doorway's

the deadline, boys! Call my hand if you figger it's bluff!"

"Use your head, Trotter! We don't want to hurt you!"

"You heard me!" Trotter warned.

Dike grinned mirthlessly. He'd seen three blow-offs like this. Each time the crowd had got its man. When they got steamed up a little more, they'd make a rush.

Out in the night beyond the window a gun barked. Dike ducked and cursed as a bullet clanged off a cell bar. He'd forgotten he was showing himself.

The deputy came in without a gun. Even his holster was empty. He was pale as he put out the oil lamp in its bracket on the wall. "Trotter says to turn you loose," he said huskily as he scraped his key against the lock.

"He's a white man."

"Hell, it ain't Trotter. Judge Claggett sent the papers over by Jake Dodge, his clerk. Jake says Izzy Blumenstein put up ten thousand dollars for your appearance in court when your case is called."

"Izzy done that?"

"God knows why," the deputy grunted as he opened the door. "Don't try to jump me. I left my gun with Trotter. The money ain't gettin' you out. Sim Beasley told the judge that Felix Morton said last night he was ridin' out to meet you in the pass an' settle an old score. Accordin' to Beasley, Morton said there might be shootin'. With Beasley sayin' that, you got a perfect case of self-defense. An' the judge is lettin' you out on that before the crowd hangs you tonight. But if you hightail for good, Izzy loses his ten thousand. You must've made medicine over Izzy."

"Sim Beasley is outta his head. That don't sound like him," Dike muttered.

"Well, he done it. I'm lettin' you sneak out the back way, ain't I?"

205

"There's a bunch hid out back in the shadows."

"It's your only chance. The crowd'll never believe Sim Beasley's story until they cool down. If you stay here, you'll hang sure as rain makes mud."

"Gimme your hat an' a broom," Dike grated. "Maybe they won't be lookin' for me to walk out back alone. I'll take the chance."

The ground sloped down from the street. They had to go down steps to reach the barred back door. The deputy cautiously peered out.

"All clear," he said huskily.

Sombrero cocked on his head, broom stuck across his arm like a gun, Dike walked out into the moonlight. His skin prickled. In the moonlight he made a perfect target. A board fence bounded the left side of the property. He could see against the fence the dark blobs that were crouching men.

Guns were on him, he knew, as he walked to the corner of the jail building and looked about. Then, stepping around out of sight, he dropped the broom on the ground and walked unhurriedly toward the street, keeping cover from the crowd milling around before the jail.

His hat pulled low, Dike walked across the street and on through another lot. Now he could rustle a horse and ride. Instead, he strode fast to the back of Beasley's law office.

A light was burning inside. A saddled horse was tied out back. Listening at the lighted window, Dike heard someone pacing back and forth inside. The door was locked. He knocked. The pacing stopped.

"Who's there?" Sim Beasley demanded nervously beyond the door.

"Kennedy."

He was admitted. The door was closed as soon as he stepped in.

Sim Beasley had a sharp nose and a dry, narrow mouth with almost bloodless lips. His ears were big and set close to his head, and his bright, beady eyes were jumpy with nervousness. "I didn't think you'd get out so easy!" he exclaimed. "Did anyone see you come here?"

"No. What's the idea of gettin' me out, Beasley?"

Sim Beasley sighed. "It's my duty to uphold both the law an' justice, Kennedy. Felix was my partner, but I had to do right as I saw right. I may suffer. I've a horse ready to ride if hotheads turn against me for my part in this."

"You wouldn't know right an' justice if you met 'em on a two-foot trail," Dike said coldly. "Spit it out, you leathernecked little fox. You're up to something, and, whatever it is, it's bound to be crooked."

Sim Beasley looked hurt. "You misjudge me, young man. Only Felix and I know what passed between us last night. Felix is beyond hurt now. I don't think you killed him. My conscience is clear in anything I've done. You show little gratitude."

"I'll talk gratitude when I get the truth. Your conscience ain't any bigger'n a dried snake rattle. What makes you think I didn't slit Morton's throat?"

Sim Beasley's eyes were very beady, very bright. "I know why Felix went out to see you, Kennedy. It wasn't a killing matter. His life was safe at your hands."

"But you lied to get me out?"

Beasley tapped his teeth with the end of a fingernail. "Felix made you an offer. *I* can still profit by it."

"Now we've got the sign on the trail. So that's how the turkey flies."

"When Trane Lamar had you whipped, he drew stakes in a gunfight. If it suits you to kill him, that's your business now," Beasley suggested slyly. He was nervous, watchful, eager.

"Tricks that ain't in the law book," Dike marveled. "Yep . . . you're smart, Beasley. But I'm out . . . which is good enough right now. I want a gun."

"Here." Eagerly Beasley opened a desk drawer and took out a belt, holster and gun, all new.

Dike strapped on the belt, spun the cylinder. "Even had it loaded, you mangy little fox. Do you know where Trane Lamar is?"

Beasley's reply was hurried and willing. "He was at the Red Dog Saloon a little while ago. Some of his men are with him. You'd better watch out for 'em."

Dike nodded, considering. "Who do you think killed Morton?" he questioned.

Sim Beasley sighed and spread his hands in a gesture of helplessness. "How could I know? Felix and I have made enemies. I've been wondering. . . ."

"Spit it out."

Sim Beasley wet his lips. "Bart Clagg followed Bud out of town that night. Trotter couldn't prove anything that would hold in court. But if you get Clagg, too, you'll have the man who killed Bud for Trane Lamar. After Lamar got the Wagon Spoke, he made Clagg foreman. Figure it out for yourself."

"Is Bart Clagg in town, too?" Dike gritted.

Before Beasley could answer, Dike swiftly cocked the gun —then lowered the muzzle as Carole Lamar came through the back door.

VI

"TO THE LAST SHELL"

Carole backed against the closing door. She was pale. "Dike. I . . . I didn't know you'd gotten out so soon."

"I'm out," Dike said harshly. There seemed nothing more to say.

Carole's eyes were on his gun. "What . . . what are you going to do now, Dike?"

"You guess."

She knew. She had difficulty forming the words: "Dike, please . . . you *can't* do that."

"Do you want to see my back?" Dike asked evenly.

Hunched and tense, Sim Beasley was watching them, but for them at that moment the little shyster did not exist.

"When you taunted him about Bud, you struck the one thing that can make him blind angry, Dike. I can't excuse what he did. He was cruelly unjust. If I could help it, I . . . I would."

"You can't."

"No," Carole said, reddening, "I see that I can't. You haven't changed much after all, have you? You're still hot-headed and reckless. You came back to revenge the rumors you'd heard about Bud. The chance that you might be wronging an innocent man didn't mean anything. Yet, when he wronged you, all you can think of is to k-kill him."

"Words," Dike said bleakly, "aren't helpin' any."

"If . . . if you go out of here with that gun, Dike, I'll spread the word you're a mad dog loose and fit only for killing."

From inside his vest Dike brought out a small picture, dog-eared, worn, and faded. It landed on the floor, face up, between them—a girl standing by her horse's head, laughing.

"Dike . . . have you had that all these years?"

"I don't want it any more," Dike said coldly. "You can spread the word quicker by goin' out the front way"

He slammed the door as he went out.

Not until he was on Sim Beasley's horse did he remember that he hadn't found why Carole had slipped into Beasley's office by the back door. There was no time to go back. The office window was already dark, and the side door of the Ventana Bar next door was opening and stabbing light out at him.

A man coming out peered at him and yelled: "Here's Dike Kennedy! He's out!"

A gun barked as Dike spurred the horse into a gallop. The horse swerved from a hit. Dike shot at the doorway, and the man dodged back, crying his discovery. Pursuit would quickly be swarming after him. Beasley's horse ran a hundred yards and fell. Dike lit running and kept on.

He still had a chance to get another horse and ride for it. Instead, grim and hard, he sought the back of the Red Dog Saloon.

A Mexican wearing a dirty white apron stood by the doorway, smoking.

"Trane Lamar in there?"

"Yes. *Dios*. . . ."

"Shut up. Turn around. Walk in ahead of me."

They went through the empty back room into the bigger bar room. Seven men were there, four of whom Dike recognized as Circle Z men. Trane Lamar stood at the bar moodily turning a whisky glass in his fingers as he talked to High-Low

Casey. High-Low was older, fatter, grayer than he'd been seven years before. He looked around as the steps entered, and stared as if he saw a ghost.

Lamar looked—and uttered a startled oath as Dike elbowed the Mexican aside.

"Anybody goin' for his gun?" Dike said coldly.

A chair clattered to the floor as Bart Clagg sprang to his feet. All hands went up. Clagg grated: "I knew somethin' like this'd happen."

Lamar slowly drank his whisky. He looked bleak and controlled. "It's happened," he said. "So you're out, Kennedy!"

"I'm out," Dike said. The wire hardness in his voice sent several of the Circle Z riders edging back. "I'm goin' to kill you now, Lamar, like I promised."

Trane Lamar smiled coldly. "We're unarmed, Kennedy."

High-Low Casey's moon face was glistening with perspiration. "For God's sake, Dike, you can't do it. They ain't heeled. You never was that kind."

Dike cursed them, savagely, bitterly. "What kind of a trick is this, Lamar?"

Trane Lamar smiled bleakly. "I heard there might be a lynchin' tonight. I wanted no part in it. I made my men turn their irons in to Trotter."

"You figgered the law'd hang me, anyway, so you stayed in the clear . . . like you did in Bud's murder."

"Damn you, Kennedy. My hands are clean on that."

"They would be. You weren't man enough to do it yourself. You hired it done. Did you promise Clagg he'd be made foreman after Bud was dead?"

Clagg's squarish head came up like a surly bull, scenting danger.

Lamar caught it. His eyes narrowed. "What's backin' up that remark, Kennedy?"

"I found out tonight Clagg followed Bud out of Palomar that night. It's enough for me."

Trane Lamar turned his back to the bar. "Bart, you were in town that day. Did you come back by the Wagon Spoke road?"

"That's two years ago. I don't remember."

"Did you kill Bud Kennedy?"

"Hell, no."

Clagg's right hand, level at the shoulder, gave a slight forward jerk. Dike swayed as the tiny Derringer Clagg had palmed blasted its dull, deadly report. The big caliber bullet had smashed his shoulder. Then Dike's roaring gun drove Clagg to the floor.

Blood bathed Dike's shoulder. The Mexican had fled. High-Low Casey had ducked down behind the bar. Dike's voice shook with fury. "You played a dirty trick on me, Lamar! I can't kill you with your hands up!"

"That's more than I expected," Lamar said.

Just then a man who seemed not to have heard the shots shoved one of the swinging doors partly open. "Izzy Blumenstein put up money to turn that skunk Kennedy loose! They're gonna hang Izzy instead! Come on!" He pulled back and ran on.

Trane Lamar said violently: "The damned fools! They've lost their heads!"

"Over against the wall, all of you," Dike ordered.

Lamar obeyed with the rest, and Dike paused at the front door. "Don't come out until you're sure I'm gone." He swung out with his gun covering the street.

He'd guessed right. The hanging of Izzy Blumenstein had drawn everyone in sight. The tumult of the crowd was retreating toward the east side of town.

Circle Z horses were at the hitch rack. Dike had the reins

of the end horse when a small figure scuttled out of the shadows.

"Kennedy?"

"Beasley, huh? D'you know they've got Izzy?"

"Yes, yes . . . what about Lamar?"

"He ain't packin' a gun. I can't shoot him," Dike said.

"You . . . you let *that* stop you?"

"Outta the way, damn you!"

Dike almost rode the lawyer down as he spurred away. Blood was dripping off his wrist. Pain was beginning to shoot through torn muscles. "You're a damn fool!" he told himself savagely.

Beasley was right. He should have killed Trane Lamar. His chances of living to meet Lamar again were pinching out. No matter. That maddened bunch couldn't string up Izzy, who'd been a friend to most of them, who'd done nothing worse than risk his money for a friend he hadn't seen in years.

The lights were still on in Izzy's deserted store. A window was broken. By morning, when angers cooled, when heads cleared, men in that crowd would be ashamed. But that wouldn't help Izzy. Dike reloaded the gun as he rode hard after them.

They had followed the dry bed of Teapot Creek down to the railroad trestle. Already a rope had been dropped over a trestle beam. Izzy was on a horse, under the trestle, his arms tied behind.

Izzy's wild pleading cut through the night. "It's a joke, ain't it, boys? I've always treated everyone right, ain't I?"

An angry voice answered: "You got Kennedy out, didn't you? It'll be the last time you meddle like that! Swing him off, boys!"

They were about to put the noose over Izzy's head when

213

Dike fired into the air and drove his horse through the fringe of the crowd.

He got the instant confusion he wanted. Men cried out, ducked, and swore. Those on foot scattered as the mounted ones spurred around to see what was happening.

Through the confusion, Dike rammed a way to Izzy. His rearing horse knocked the man with the noose aside. A sweep of his arm slammed Izzy across the saddle in front of him. His gun blazing high, but viciously, opened a path through the men ahead.

Gunshots behind went wild in confusion, but more guns opened up as Dike rode hard up the creekbank. Looking back, he saw riders breaking out from under the trestle after them. Izzy kicked, cried out as a bullet hit him.

They plunged over the lip of the bank to a moment's safety. But only a moment. Dike knew they couldn't pull away from the riders behind.

A small adobe house squatted dark and silent ahead. Beyond it were other scattered houses where some of the Palomar Mexicans lived. Izzy staggered as Dike slid him to the ground behind the first little hut.

"I got a bullet in my leg," Izzy moaned. "Dike, it *is* you, ain't it?"

Dike jumped for the back door. "Get in here. I'll do what I can for you, but it ain't much."

The hut had two little rooms. The back room was still warm from the supper fire. The occupants had evidently left when they heard the crowd down in the dry creekbed.

Dike fired through a window glass at a rider outside. The horse swerved and bolted away. Other men galloped for cover, throwing shots back at the house as they went.

"Look around for a gun," Dike panted.

Izzy spoke excitedly as he groped about the room.

214

"Someone came with you, didn't they, Dike? Tom Trotter or someone?"

"Nope." Dike stepped aside from the window as a rifle bullet smashed the glass.

"You . . . you came alone after me?" Izzy asked weakly.

"That's right. You got into this by helpin' me, didn't you?"

"Yes," Izzy groaned, "an' no, Dike. I tried to help you this afternoon by knockin' you out before they killed you. But it was Carole Lamar who got you out."

"*What?*"

"Here's an old belt and gun hangin' on the wall," Izzy quavered. "What'll I do with it?"

"Damn the gun! What'd Carole do?"

"She came to me an' said there was talk of lynchin' you, an' she'd been to Sim Beasley, an' he told her he could get you out, but it'd take money. She told me her father didn't have any . . . she couldn't get it."

"How much did she think she'd get if he did have it?" Dike rasped sarcastically.

Izzy quavered: "I told her the Lamar holdings were good enough for me, if Trane'd sign for part of it. I never thought you killed Morton, Dike. Last evening I saw Sim an' Felix ride out of town together. Sim didn't tell anyone about that. It looked funny to me."

"So Beasley left town with Morton. Did you tell the sheriff?"

"I didn't know anything for sure, Dike. I thought I'd wait an' see what happened. It ain't good business to hunt trouble. But when there was talk of hangin' you, an' Trane Lamar came back with Carole an' signed for seven thousand dollars, I went with Beasley to the judge an'. . . ."

"Are you telling me Trane Lamar went on my bond?"

Dike yelled violently as he emptied his gun out the opposite window.

Through the powder reek, into concussion-ringing ears, Izzy's reply came thinly. "He signed for part of it, Dike. An' then they come to hang me for it. Is that reasonable, I ask you?"

"None of it's reasonable!" Dike exploded. "Get back in the other room an' watch that window an' door!"

Izzy may have had some hope as he limped into the back room. Dike did not. When the slim supply of cartridges gave out, they were through. A score and more of men had gone to cover around the little hut.

A man could go heartsick at the uselessness of trying to reason now with those men outside. He could despair at the hopelessness of getting them to see that, if Sim Beasley had left town with Felix Morton the previous night and had said nothing about it afterwards, then Sim Beasley knew who had killed Morton. Only one man could have done it. Sim Beasley himself. Tricky to the last, Felix Morton had lied there in the San Gabriel Pass when he said no one had come with him. Somewhere off in the darkness Sim Beasley had been waiting, listening.

Guns were hammering, crashing in the night. Bullets were splintering through the doors, smashing the windows, thudding into the adobe walls. Izzy's gun blasted in the back room.

Dike dodged from window to window, nursing his supply of cartridges while his mind grappled with the tangled skein of events that had made this homecoming one straight run of hell.

Trane Lamar had nursed a dislike for seven years—and then offered the ultimate insult and injury. Then, broke as he was in this time of drought, Lamar had put his name to a note for thousands. You hardly could believe a thing like that. Beasley hadn't said anything about it. But Beasley wouldn't. His mind and ways were too devious and crooked. Granted that he'd killed his partner for reasons of his own and left the knife there to cast the blame on the returning prodigal, then Beasley had turned right around and lied about Morton, and used Lamar's money to get that same prodigal out of jail—in order that the prodigal would head for Trane Lamar and kill him.

Beasley had told just enough to suit his ends. No more. Not until Felix Morton's disclosures were taken into account did much of it have any sense. Then you saw—as Dike saw amidst flaming guns and growing hopelessness—that it was all part of the web Morton and Beasley had been weaving for control of the Circle Z range.

When that was plain, there was not much room left for the hating of anyone else. Long-lasting emotions, that had hardened and died under the bite of Trane Lamar's whip, stirred and grew warm again. But it was all hopeless. The thin supply of cartridges was fast dwindling, and only flaming guns would talk to that excited, blood-maddened, mistaken, and misunderstanding crowd out there in the night.

VII
"FIGHTING MEN—BACK TO BACK"

Here and there, unseen in vagrant shadows, a man had crept closer, answering with increasing quickness the gun flashes at the window. A bullet clipped Dike's ear. Another knocked glass splinters into his face. Blood began to drip down his cheek. His left arm had been bleeding steadily. The artery had been missed, but the steady seep of blood was fast sapping strength. Dike could feel himself getting light-headed.

Izzy's yell of fright sounded fainter, much farther off, than it should have.

"I'm hit in the arm, Dike! They're up close to the back of the house!"

"Hold 'em off!"

"I only got three more cartridges!" Izzy wailed.

Dike staggered a little as he went in and gave Izzy four cartridges. "That's all you get," he warned. "Keep away from the door."

Through the shattered window Dike made out several dark patches on the ground, where no shadow should be. He fired at one. A man jumped up and broke for safety. Others followed.

Dike let them go. There were no cartridges to spare.

"It's comin' in a few minutes now, Izzy," he said. "You might as well know it."

Izzy was silent for a moment. "All right, Dike. Maybe I'll save one shot. It's easier than a rope." He limped closer and touched Dike's arm. His voice was husky. "I never was much, Dike. Just a little cow-town storekeeper that everybody cussed out when they felt like it. Sometimes it hurt, too. I was proud of my business like they was proud of their cows an' land. But I liked 'em, Dike, even when they didn't pay their bills. They was my customers. We were all livin' together an' workin' to get somewhere. I don't know where we were tryin' to get, Dike. Bigger an' better before we died, I guess. It looks like I'm gonna die now. An' I'm scared. Scared as hell. But I'd put up money an' go to the judge again. Your family was good customers, Dike, an' I always tried to carry my customers through."

Dike put his arm across Izzy's thin shoulder. "Damn you, Izzy, you're a better man than any skunk out there. I'm proud I know you."

Izzy gulped. "That makes me feel mighty good, Dike."

"Get over in the corner there," Dike ordered gruffly. "Don't shoot until you see a man comin' through the door or fillin' up the window. Then *get* him! I hate to kill off the fools . . . but they're askin' for it. So long, Izzy."

"So long, Dike."

Swearing to himself, Dike went back into the front room. Funny how a little scrabbly storekeeper who tried to see his customers through could bring a lump in your throat. Not a man out there but was dealing himself a loss in this night's work. Mob-like, they were merely following blind impulse now—and, when they woke up, it would be too late.

With the cessation of fire from the adobe hut, the men outside became bolder. Dark form after dark form edged nearer in the moonlight.

Dike yelled out the window: "We're waitin' for the first half dozen of you fools to make a rush! You could hang a helpless devil bold enough! Run up an' shoot it out with him!"

"That you, Kennedy?"

"Who d'you think it is?"

The same voice said: "Walk out here like a man an' we'll let Izzy go!"

"I'd take you up on that if I was dealin' with a bunch of men!"

"This is Ben James talkin'! I'm passin' my word on it! How about it, boys?" James yelled.

A chorus of agreement answered him. "To hell with Izzy, if we get Kennedy!"

"Dike, you ain't gonna do it," Izzy burst out from the doorway.

Dike, opening the front door, said: "Sit pat, Izzy. A good customer's got to pay his bill sometime. Here's mine . . . an' good luck to you."

"*Dike!*" Izzy wailed.

"Watch yourselves! I'm comin'!" Dike yelled as he lunged out into the night.

But his legs were wobbly. He couldn't run as he wanted to. He saw men dodging out into the moonlight and running toward him. Ahead of him some man's jumpy nerves set off a gun.

Dike fired at the flash and kept on, but, as if that were a signal, other guns opened up. Hanging was forgotten. All they wanted now was to pot him like an escaping rabbit. His gun clicked on empty. Dike thumbed in his last shells as he plunged on through that gauntlet of gunfire.

Through the blasting of six-shooters he heard the drumming roll of galloping horses coming up fast behind him. They were going to ride him down. Then a bullet struck his leg, and he sprawled forward on his face. He'd held onto his gun, and groggily he rolled over to fight it out to the last bullet.

He saw the riders coming, eight or nine of them storming through the moonlight around the adobe hut, spreading out, lacing the night with shots and shouting. But the gun flashes were aimed up, and the words Dike caught didn't make sense.

"Hold your fire! Hold it!"

The encircling guns went silent. The snorting horses were reined in. A loud voice challenged: "This is Sheriff Trotter talkin'! The party's over! I've got a posse deputized an' ordered to shoot to kill! Where's Izzy?"

A second, cold voice followed: "This is Trane Lamar of the Circle Z! Sim Beasley just tried to kill me! Before he died, he confessed killin' Felix Morton out in the pass with Kennedy's knife! We've found the man who killed Bud Kennedy! You men have made one hell of a mistake! Don't make it worse by losin' your heads now!"

One stricken voice made reply, and it was an answer for the rest: "My God, we've done kilt one innocent man an' almost got another."

The crowd started to melt away, running furtively for their horses, diving for the nearest shadows and a getaway before their identities were unmasked.

Little Izzy staggered out into the moonlight, calling: "Dike? Did they get you, Dike?"

"What's that? Is Kennedy here?" Trane Lamar called loudly.

"They said, if he'd come out, they'd let me go," Izzy groaned wildly. "An' he ran out, an' they opened up on him. They must've killed him. That's him there on the ground. See him."

Trane Lamar galloped ahead of the other riders toward the spot. He hit the ground running, as Dike lurched to his feet.

"Kennedy?"

"It's me."

"You ain't dead?"

"Do I look it?" Dike said. "So Beasley tried to get you himself, did he?"

"He was a poor shot," Lamar replied dryly. "He hit the man next to me in the arm. I had a gun by then an' drilled him in the shadows where he was hidin'. When Doc Rumboldt told him he was dyin', he talked. Seems him an' Morton have been hatin' each other for a long time. Beasley hired Bart

Clagg to get your brother, an' Clagg held it over him after I cut 'em out buyin the Wagon Spoke. Morton blamed him for bein' fool enough to trust Clagg. Each had been waitin' to do the other dirt an' knew it, so when Beasley seen a chance to slit Morton's throat and lay the blame on you, he took it, figurin' he could fix up a lot of other things the same way. Bart Clagg talked, too, before he died. We'd 'a' been here sooner, but all that an' gettin' our guns, held us up."

"Izzy told me you signed my bond, Lamar. It don't jibe. I been wonderin'."

The other men were around them by that time. Trane Lamar hesitated, and then spoke gruffly, as if ashamed of the confession. "I lost my head today. Carole brought me to my senses. She reminded me how I'd been blamed for Bud's death, an' how I felt when I knew I was innocent. An' she swore you never would have cut any man's throat, an' I couldn't let you hang for that." Gruffly Lamar added: "Sometimes I'm hard, but I try to be fair. Signin' my name was the least I could do. I ain't askin' your pardon for what I ordered done. But you've proved up a man to me tonight, Kennedy. A better man than I've been, I guess. You're welcome at the Circle Z. I'll be proud to be your friend, if you ever feel like it."

"I'm shot up," Dike said. "If the Circle Z has got an extra bed until I'm well, friend, I'll be grateful."

"Your bed's waitin' now, Dike. Here, lemme help you."

"You might," said Dike, as he took Trane Lamar's big hand, "tell Carole I'm comin'."

Trane Lamar chuckled. "I won't have to," he said. "She's waitin'."

"Let's go," said Dike.

ABOUT THE AUTHOR

T. T. Flynn was born Thomas Theodore Flynn, Jr., in Indianapolis, Indiana. He was the author of over a hundred Western short novels for such leading pulp magazines as Street & Smith's *Western Story Magazine*, Popular Publications' *Dime Western*, and Dell's *Zane Grey's Western Magazine*. He lived much of his life in New Mexico and spent much of his time on the road, exploring the vast terrain of the American West. His descriptions of the land are always detailed, but he used them not only for local color but also to reflect the heightening of emotional distress among the characters within a story. Following the Second World War, Flynn turned his attention to the book-length Western novel and in this form also produced work that has proven imperishable. Five of these novels first appeared as original paperbacks, most notably THE MAN FROM LARAMIE (1954) which was also featured as a serial in *The Saturday Evening Post* and subsequently made into a memorable motion picture directed by Anthony Mann and starring James Stewart, and TWO FACES WEST (1954) which deals with the problems of identity and reality and served as the basis for a television series. He was highly innovative and inventive and in later novels, such as NIGHT OF THE COMANCHE MOON (Five Star Westerns, 1995), concentrated on deeper psychological issues as the source for conflict, rather than more elemental motives like greed. Flynn is at his best in stories that combine mystery—not surprisingly, he also wrote detective fiction—with suspense and action in an artful balance. The psychological dimensions of Flynn's Western fiction came increasingly to encompass a confrontation with ethical principles about how one must live, the values that one must hold dear above all else, and his belief that there must be a balance in all things. The cosmic meaning of the mortality of all living creatures had become for him a unifying metaphor for the fragility and dignity of life itself. HELL'S CAÑON is his next **Five Star Western**.